"*A*wfully nice of you to come," said the Rev. Sir Rufus to the dragon.

There was a rather awkward pause.

"You must be hungry," said the Rev. Sir Rufus. "Some roast sow, perhaps? Roast boar?"

The dragon Smarasderagd showed his teeth. The crowd retreated. "*Flesh*?" screamed the dragon. "Good heavens, it gives me heartburn . . ."

The crowd breathed a sigh of relief. Prince Peregrine, however, emitted a slight chuckle . . .

PEREGRINE SECUNDUS

THE HUGO AWARD WINNER'S EPIC JOURNEY TO THE LIGHTER SIDE OF THE DARK AGES

PEREGRINE: SECUNDUS

by AVRAM DAVIDSON

BERKLEY BOOKS, NEW YORK

The first portion of this book appeared in *The Magazine of Fantasy and Science Fiction* in October 1973, under the title of *Peregrine: Alflandia*. The second half of the book appeared in *Isaac Asimov's Science Fiction Magazine* in October 1980, under the title of *Peregrine: Perplexed*.

PEREGRINE SECUNDUS

A Berkley Book / published by arrangement with
the author

PRINTING HISTORY
Berkley edition / May 1981
Second printing / September 1981

ISBN: 0-425-04829-2

A BERKLEY BOOK ® TM 757,375

PRINTED IN THE UNITED STATES OF AMERICA

Acknowledgement and Absolution

AVRAM DAVIDSON DECLARES:

"All of the Umbrian words and some of the English ones are to be found in a massive work of immense scholarship, *The Bronze Tablets of Iguvium*, by James Wilson Poultney, published in 1959 by the American Philological Society and the Johns Hopkins University Press, Baltimore, none of whom are in any way responsible for the use which Mr. Davidson has made of this material. And he has made some pretty free use."

The author wishes to express his thanks to Karen Anderson for her gracious gift of the name *Smarasderagd*, and to the Rev. Mr. Hisao Niwa and the Rev. Mrs. Masako Niwa of the Tenrikyo Hope of the Pacific Fellowship for so kindly having lent the space in which much of this book was written.

The King of the Alves was taking his evening rest and leisure after a typical hard day's work ferreting in the woods behind the donjeon-keep, which—in Alfland—was a goodish distance from the Big House. It was usual, of course, for the donjeon-keep to be kept as part and parcel of the Big House, but the Queen of Alfland had objected to the smell.

"It's them drains, me dear," her lord had pointed out to her more than once when she made these objections. "The High King isn't due to make a Visitation this way for another half-a-luster, as well you know. And also as well you know what'd likely happen to me if I was to infringe upon the High Royal Monopoly and do my own plumbing on them drains, a mere pettyking like me."

"I'd drains him, if I was a man," said the Queen of Alfland. "*And* the prices as he charges, too! 'Tisn't as if he was contented with three peppercorns and a stewed owl in a silver tassy, like his father before him; ah! *There* was a High King for you! Well, well, I see it can't be helped, having wedded a mouse instead of a proper man; well, then *move* the wretched donjeon-keep, it doesn't pay for itself no-how, and if it wasn't as our position requires we have one, blessed if I'd put up with it.''

So the donjeon-keep had been laboriously taken down and laboriously removed and laboriously set up again just this side of the woods; and there, of a very late afternoon, the King of the Alves sat on a hummock with his guest, the King of Bertland. Several long grey ears protruded from a sack at their feet, and now and then a red-eyed ferret poked his snouzel out of a royal pocket and was gently poked back in. The Master of the Buckhounds sat a short ways aways, a teen-age boy who was picking the rem-nants of a scab off one leg and meditatively crunch-ing the pieces between his teeth. He was Alfland's son and heir; there were of course not really any buckhounds.

''Well, Alf, you hasn't done too bad today,'' the royal guest observed after a while.

''No, I hasn't, Bert, and that's a fact. Stew for the morrow, and one day at a time is all any man dare look for to attend to and haccomplish, way *I* look at it.'' The day was getting set to depart in a sort of silver-gilt haze, throstles were singing *twit-twit-thrush*, and swallows were flitting back and forth pretending they were bats. The Master of the Buckhounds arose.

''Hey, Da, is they any bread and cheese more?'' he asked.

''No, they isn't, Buck. Happen thee'll get thy dinner soon enough.''

The Master of the Buckhounds said that he was going to see could he find some berries or a muskroom and sauntered off into the thicket. His sire nudged the guest. "Gone to play with hisself, I'll be bound," said he.

"Why don't 'ee marry 'im off?" asked the King of Bertland, promptly. "There's our Rose, has her hope chest all filled and still as chaste as the day the wise woman slapped her newborn bottom, ten year ago last Saturnalia, eh?"

The King of the Alves grunted moodily. "Hasn't I sudggestered this to his dam?" he asked, rhetorically. " 'Here's Bert come for to marry off his datter,' says I, 'for thee doesn't think there's such a shortage o' rabbiting in Bertland he have to come here for it, whatever the formalities of it may be. And Princess Rose be of full age and can give thee a hand in the kitching,' says I. But, no, says she. For why? Buck haven't gone on no quest nor haven't served no squire time at the High King's court and ten-year-old is too old-fashioned young and he be but a boy hisself and she don't need no hand in the kitching and if I doesn't like the way me victuals be served, well, I can go and eat beans with the thralls, says she.

"Well, do she natter that Buck have pimples, 'twill serve she right, say I. Best be getten back. Ar, these damp edgerows will give me the rheum in me 'ips, so we sit 'ere more, eh?"

He hefted his sack of hares and they started back. The King of Bertland gestured to the donjeon-keep, where a thin smoke indicated the warder was cooking his evening gruel. "As yer ransomed off King Baldwin's heir as got tooken in the humane man-trap last winter what time 'e sought to 'unt the tusky boar?"

The walls of Alftown came into sight, with the same *three breeches and a rent* which characterized

the walls of every castle and capital town as insisted
on by Wilfredoric Conqueror, the late great-uncle of
the last High King but one. Since that time, Alfish (or
Alvish, as some had it) royalty had been a-dwelling in
a Big House, which was contained behind a stout
stockade: this, too, was customary.

"What, didn't I notify you about that, Bert?"
the Alf-king asked, with a slightly elaborate air of
surprise. "Ah, many's the good joke and jest we've
had about that in the fambly, *'Da has tooken King
Baldy's hair, harharharhar!'* Yus, the old man finally
paid up, three mimworms and a dragon's egg.
*'Mustn't call him King Baldy now he's got his heir
back, horhorhorhor!'* Ah, what's life wiffart larfter?
Or, looking hat it another way, wiffart *h*honor: we
was meaning to surprise you, Bert, afore you left, by
putten them mimworms and that dragon's hegg hinto
a suitable container wif a nice red ribbon and say,
'Ere you be, King o' Bertland, hand be pleased to
haccept this as your winnings for that time we played
forfeits last time we played it.' Surprise yer, yer see.
But now yer've spoiled that helement of it; ah, well,
must take the bitter wif the sweet."

That night after dinner the three mimworms and
the dragon's egg were lifted out from the royal
hidey-hole and displayed for the last time at Alf
High-Table before being taken off to their new
home. Princess Pearl and Princess Ruby gave over
their broidered-work, and young Buck (he was
officially Prince Rufus but was never so called)
stopped feeding scruffles to his bird and dog—a
rather mangy-looking mongrel with clipped claws—
and Queen Clara came back out of the kitchen.

"Well, this is my last chance, I expect," said
Princess Pearl, a stout good-humored young girl,

with rather large feet. "Da, give us thy ring."

"Ar, this time, our Pearl, happen thee'll have luck," her sire said, indulgently; and he took off his finger the Great Sigil-Stone Signet-Ring of the Realm, which he occasionally affixed to dog licenses and the minutes of the local wardmotes, and handed it to her. Whilst the elders chuckled indulgently and her brother snorted and her baby sister looked on with considerable envy, the elder princess began to make the first mystic sign—and then, breaking off, said, "Well, now, and since it *is* the last chance, do thee do it for me, our Ruby, as I've 'ad no luck a-doin' it for meself so far—"

Princess Ruby clapped her hands. "Oh, *may* I do it, oh, please, please, our Pearl? Oh, you are *good* to me! Ta ever so!" and she began the ancient game with her cheeks glowing with delight and expectation:

> *Mimworm dim, mimworm bright,*
> *Make the wish I wish tonight:*
> *By dragon egg and royal king,*
> *Send now for spouse the son of a king!*

The childish voice and gruff chuckles were suddenly all drowned out by screams, shouts, cries of astonishment, and young Buck's anguished wail; for where his bird had been, safely jessed, there suddenly appeared a young man as naked as the day of his birth.

Fortunately the table had already been cleared, and, nakedness not ever having been as fashionable in East Brythonia (the largest island in the Black Sea) as it had been in parts farther south and west, the young man was soon rendered as decent as the second-best tablecloth could make him.

"Our Pearl's husband! Our Pearl's husband! See, I *did* do it right, *look*! Our Mum and our Da, *look*!" and Princess Ruby clapped her hands together. King Alf and King Bert sat staring and muttering . . . perhaps charms, or countercharms . . . Buck, with tears in his eyes, demanded his bird back, but without much in his tone to indicate that he held high hopes . . . Princess Pearl had turned and remained a bright, bright red . . . and Queen Clara stood with her hands on her hips and her lips pressed together and a face—as her younger daughter put it later: "O Lor! Wasn't Mum's face a study!"

Study or no, Queen Clara said now, "Well, and pleased to meet this young man, I'm sure, but it seems to me there's more to this than meets the heye. Our Pearl is still young for all she's growed hup into a fine young 'oman, and I don't know as I'm all that keen on 'er marrying someone as we knows nuffink abahrt, hexcept that 'e use ter be a bird; look at that there 'Elen of Troy whose dad was a swan, Leda was 'er mum's name; what sort of 'ome life d'you think she could of 'ad, no better than they should be, the two of them, mother and daughter—what! Alfland! Yer 'as some'at to say, 'as yer!" She turned fiercely on her king, who had indeed been mumbling something about live and let live, and it takes all kinds, and seems a gormly young man: "Ah, and if another Trojan War is ter start, needn't think to take Buck halong and—"

But she had gone too far.

"Nah then, nah then, Queen Clara," said her king. "Seems to me yer've gotten things fair muddled, that 'ere Trojing War come abaht acause the lady herself 'ad more nor one 'usband, an' our Pearl 'asn't—leastways not as *I* knows of. First yer didn't want Buck to get married, nah yer wants our Pearl ter stay at 'ome. I dessay, when it come our Ruby's time, yer'll 'ave some'at to say 'bout that, too. Jer want me line, the royal line-age o' the Kings of Alfland, as as come down from King Deucalion's days, ter die aht haltergether?'' And to this the queen had no word to utter, or, at least, none she thought it prudent to; so her husband turned to the young man clad in the second-best tablecloth (the best, of course, always being saved for the lustral Visitations of the High King himself)—and rather well did he look in it, too—and said, ''Sir, we bids yer welcome to this 'ere 'Igh Table, which it's mine, King Earwig of Alfland is me style and title, not but what I mightn't 'ave another, nottersay other *ones*, if so be I 'ad me entitles and me right. Ah, 'ad not the King o' the Norf, Arald Ardnose, slain Earl Oscaric the Ostrogoth at Slowstings, thus allowing Juke Wilfred of Southmandy to hobtain more than a mere foot'old, as yer might call it, this 'ud be a united kingdom today instead of a mere patch'ork quilt of petty kingdomses. Give us an account of yerself, young man, as yer hobliged to do hanyway according to the lore.''

And at once proceeded to spoil the effect of this strict summons by saying to his royal guest, ''Pour us a drain o' malt and one for this young sprig, wonthcher, Bert,'' and handed the mug to the young sprig with his own hands and the words, '' 'Ere's what made the deacon dance, so send it down the red road, brother, and settle the dust.''

They watched the ale go rippling down the newcomer's throat, watched him smack his lips. Red glows danced upon the fire-pit hearth, now and then illuminating the path of the black smoke all the way up to the pitchy rafters where generations of other smokes had left their soots and stains. And then, just as they were wondering whether the young man had a tongue or whether he peradventure spoke another than the one in which he had been addressed, he opened his comely red lips and spoke.

"Your Royal Grace and Highnesses," he said, "and Prince and Princesses, greetings."

"Greetings," they all said, in unison, including, to her own pleased surprise, Queen Clara, who even removed her hands from under the apron embroidered with the golden crowns, where she had been clasping them tightly, and sat down, saying that the young man spoke real well and was easily seen to have been well brought hup, whatsoever 'e 'ad been a bird: but there, we can't always 'elp what do befall us in this vale of tears.

"To give an account of myself," the young man went on, after no more than a slight pause, "would be well lengthy, if complete. Perhaps it might suffice for now for me to say that as I was on the road running north and east out of Chiringirium in the Middle, or Central, Roman Empire, I was by means of a spell cast by a benevolent sorcerer, transformed into a falcon in order that I might be saved from a much worse fate; that whilst in the form of that same bird I was taken in a snare and manned by one trained in that art, by him sold or exchanged for three whippets and a brace of woodcock to a trader out of Tartary by way of the Crimea; and by *him* disposed of to a wandering merchant, who in turn made me over to this young prince here for two silver pennies and a great piece of gammon. I must say that this is very good ale," he said, enthusiastically. "The Romans don't make good ale, you know, it's all wine with them. My old dadda used to tell me,

'Perry, my boy, clean barrels and good malt make clean good ale . . .' "

And, as he recalled the very tone of his father's voice and the very smell of his favorite old cloak, and realized that he would never see him more, a single tear rolled unbidden from the young man's eye and down the down of his cheek and was lost in the tangle of his soft young beard, though not lost to the observation of all present. Buck snuffled, Ruby climbed up in the young man's lap and placed her slender arms round his neck, Queen Clara blew her nose into her gold-embroidered apron, King Bert cleared his throat, and King Alf-Earwig brushed his own eyes with his sleeve.

"Your da told yer that, eh?" he said, after a moment. "Well, he told yer right and true . . . What, call him dadda, do 'ee? Why, yer must be one a them Lower Europeans, then, for I've 'eard it's their way o' speech. What's 'is name, then—and what's yours, for that matter?"

Princess Pearl, speaking for the first time since giving the ring to her small sister, said, "Why, Da, haven't he told us that? His name is Perry." And then she blushed an even brighter red than ever.

"Ah, he have, our Pearl. I'll be forgetting my own name next. Changed into a falcon-bird and then changed back again, eh? Mind them mimworms and that 'ere dragon hegg, Bert; keep 'em safe locked hup, for where there be magic there be mischief. But what's yer guvnor's name, young Perry?"

Young Perry had had time to think. Princess Pearl was to all appearances an honest young woman and no doubt skilled in the art of spindle and distaff and broider-sticking, as befitted the daughter of a petty king; and as befitted one, she was passing eager and ready for marriage to the son of another such. But Perry had no present mind to be that son. Elliptically he answered with another question. "Have you heard of Sapodilla?"

Brows were knit, heads were scratched. Elliptics is a game at which more than one can play. "That be where you're from, then?" replied King Alf.

The answer, such as it was, was reassuring. He felt he might safely reveal a bit more without revealing too much more. "My full name, then, is Peregrine the son of Paladrine, and I *am* from Sapodilla and it *is* in Lower Europe. And my father sent me to find my older brother, Austin, who looks like me, but blond."—This was stretching the truth but little. Eagerness rising in him at the thought, he asked, "Have any of you seen such a man?"

King Bert took the answer upon himself. "Mayhap such a *bird* is what 'ee should better be a-hasking for, *horhorhor!*" he said. And then an enormous yawn lifted his equally enormous moustache.

Someone poked Perry in the side with a sharp stick. He did not exactly open his eyes and sit up, there on the heap of sheepskin and blanketure nigh the still hot heap of coals in the great hall; for somehow he knew that he was sleeping. This is often the prelude to awakening, but neither did he awake. He continued to lie there and to sleep, though aware of the poke and faintly wondering about it. And then it came again, and a bit more peremptory, and so he turned his mind's eye to it, and before his mind's eye he saw the form and figure of a man with a rather sharp face, and this one said to him, "Now, attend, and don't slumber off again, or I'll fetch you back, and perhaps a trifle less pleasantly; you are new to this island, and none come here new without my knowing it, and yet I did *not* know it. Attend, therefore, and explain.''

And Peregrine heard himself saying, in a voice rather like the buzzing of bees (and he complimented himself, in his dream, for speaking thus, for it seemed to him at that time and in that state that this was the appropriate way for him to be speaking). ''Well, and well do I now know that I have passed through either the Gate of Horn or the Gate of Ivory, but which one I know not, do you see?''

''None of that, now, that is not my concern: explain, explain, explain; what do you here and how came you here, to this place, called 'the largest island in the Black Sea,' though not truly an island . . . and, for that matter, perhaps not even truly in the Black Sea . . . Explain. Last summons.''

Perry sensed that no more prevarications were in order. ''I came here, then, sir, in the form of an hawk or falcon, to which state I was reduced by white witchery; and by white witchery was I restored to my own natural manhood after arriving.''

The sharp eyes scanned him. The sharp mouth pursed itself in more than mere words. ''Well explained, and honestly. So. I have more to do, and many cares, and I think you need not be one of them. For now I shall leave you, but know that from time to time I shall check and attend to your presence and your movements and your doings. *Sleep!*''

Again the stick touched him, but now it was more like a caress, and the rough, stiff fleece and harsh blankets felt as smooth to his naked skin as silks and downs.

He awoke again, and properly this time, to see

the grey dawnlight touched with pink. A thrall was blowing lustily upon the ember with a hollowed tube of wood and laying fresh fagots of wood upon it. An even lustier rumble of snores came from the adjacent heap of covers, whence protruded a pair of hairy feet belonging, presumably, to the King of Bertland. And crouching by his own side was Buck.

Who said, "Hi."

"Hi," said Perry, sitting up.

"You used to be a peregrine falcon and now you're a peregrine man?" the younger boy asked.

"Yes. But don't forget that I was a peregrine man before becoming a falcon. And let me thank you for the care and affection which you gave me when I was your hawk, Buck. I will try to replace myself . . . or replace the bird you've lost, but as I don't know just when I can or how, even, best I make no promise."

At this point the day got officially underway at Alfland Big House, and there entered the king himself, followed by the Lord High Great Steward, aged eight (who, having ignominiously failed his apprenticeship as kitchenboy by forgetting to turn the spit and allowing a pair of pullets to burn, had been demoted), carrying hot water and towels; the soft-soap, in a battered silver basin, being born by King Alf. He also bore an ostrich feather which had seen better days, and with this he ceremoniously tickled the feet of King Bert, whose snores ceased abruptly. The hot water and towels were set on a bench and the burnished tray set up in a convenient niche to serve as mirror. King Bert grunted greetings, took his sickle-shaped razor out of his ditty bag, and, seizing one wing of his moustache and pulling the adjacent skin out, began to shave.

"Buck," said King of the Alves, "yer mum wants yer. Nar then, young Perry," he said, "what I wants ter know is this: Haccording to the charm as our Ruby's been and done unto yer, yer supposed to be the son of a king. Sometimes magic gets muddled, has we all knows, take for hinstance that time the Conqueror 'e says to 'iz wizard, 'Conjure me up the ghost of Caesar,' not specifying *which* Caesar 'e meant but hassuming 'e'd 'ave great Caesar's ghost hand no hother, which 'e 'adn't; the resultant confusion we needn't go hinter. *However*. *'Bring now for spouse the son of a king,'* says the charm, doesn't say *which* king, do it, but meantersay: His you hor hisn't you, a fair question, lad, give us a fair hanswer."

This Peregrine felt the man was entitled to, but he was by no means delighted with the implications. "In a manner of speaking, Sir King," he said, wiggling slightly—and then, reflecting that the truth is more often the best than not, he added, "I am my father's youngest bastard son, and he has three heirs male of his body lawfully begotten."

King Alf digested this. It could almost be seen going down. "Well, then, we can homit *Prince* Peregrine, can we. Mmmm. Which means, *Queen* Pearl, we needn't look forrert to that, neither. 'Er dowery 'ud be smaller, there's a saving, right there. Nor she needn't move far away, Lower Europe, meantersay, might's well be Numidia for all the chance us'd ever get to visit. 'As a one or two by-blows meself. Fust one, wasn't never sure was it by me or was it by a peddler as'd been by 'awking plaice; lad turned fifteen, stole a fishing smack one night and run wif it: I crossed 'is name horf the Royal Genealogical Chart hand 'ad a scribe write *Denounciated hand Renounciated* hafter it. Tother un' was

the spit and image of me Huncle Percy, long afore
deceased; but this lad went to the bad just like tother
one, hexcept 'e become a physician specializing in the
infirmities of women. As yer might say. 'Ope yer
own da 'as 'ad better luck . . .''

His voice ended in a mumble, then plucked up
again. "Now, no doubt yer da has ennobled you,
give yer some such title as it might be, say, Count of
Cumtwaddle and Lord of the Three Creeks in the
peerage of Sapodilla, hey?'' he inquired, hopefully.

Peregrine sighed, shook his sleek head, informed the host-king that what his father had given
him was his blessing, a month's rations, three mules,
a suit of the best second-rate armor, and a few other
similar items; plus the ritual warning, established by
law, that it would be Death for him to return either
armed or at the head of an armed multitude.

King Alf grunted. "Well," he said, tone halfway
between disappointment and approbation, "s'pose
that's one way to preserve the loreful succession,
makes sense, too bad, well, well.'' He shook his
head. The gesture seemed to indicate bafflement
rather than a negative decision. Another grunt announced a fresh idea . . . or two.

"Well, be that as it may, Queen Clara sends her
good wishes and says please to excuse as she needs
back the tablecloth. Now, we can't 'ave yer traipsing
round in yer bare minimum, for folk 'ud larf hat us
ha-keeping hup them hold-fashioned Grecian him-
fluences. So." He displayed an armful of garments.
"One o' these is what's left o' what I've grew out of,
but maybe it be still too large. And tother is for Buck
ter grow into, maybe it be still too small. Only way to
find out is to dive and try."

Perry thanked him, dived and tried. The pair of

trews, woven in a tessellated pattern according to the old Celtish style, and intended for Buck to grow into, fit him well enough; but the tunic was a bit tight across the chest and shoulders; the tunic which Buck's father had grown out of, though an outsize round the waist, had exactly Perry's sleeve length. The same lucky fit obtained with the sandals, formerly the property of King Baldy's heir. "And here," said the royal host, setting down a casket inlaid in ivory, "is the gear box, and you may poke around for clasps, buckles, fibulae, and such; please 'elp yerself. No 'urry, hexcept that betwixt dawn and noon we as a rightchual ceremony to hattend; like ter 'ave yer wiff us."

The clepsydra at Alfland Big House had been for some time out of order, the king insisting with vigor that fixing it would constitute making plumbing repairs and thus an infringement on the High Royal Monopoly, the queen—for her part—insisting with equal vigor that the king was trying to cover up his ignorance of how to make the repairs. Be that as it may, the great water-clock remained unfixed, only now and then emitting a gurgle, a trickle, and a groan, rather like an elderly gentleman with kidney trouble. Be that as *that* may, at an hour approximately between dawn and noon, Peregrine, alerted by a minor clamor in the courtyard, made his way thither.

He saw gathered there the entire royal family and household, including thralls; the guest king, who had delayed his departure in order to witness the ritual ceremony; a number of citizens, whose abrupt discontinuance of conversation, and interested examination of Peregrine as he approached, gave him reason to believe they had been talking about him; and three archers, three slingers, and three spearmen: these last nine constituting the Army of the Realm (cavalry had been strictly forbidden by Wilfred the Conqueror).

"Ah, Peregrine the son of Paladrine the Soverereign of Sapodilla in Lower Europe," the King of the Alves announced, slightly pompously. And at once said, in his usual gruffly affable manner, "Come on over, Perry, and leave me hexplain to yer the nature of this hoccasion. See," he gestured, "that there is Thuh Treasure. Likewise, the Treasury."

"What, that single sack?" was the sentence which Perry had in mind to say, but, tactfully, did not.

King Alf continued, portentously, "Now, this is the third day hafter the full moon of the month of Hecatombaeon haccording to thuh hold Religion," he coughed delicately into his fist, "meantersay we're hall good hArians 'ere, and so naturally we've tried to git this fixed hup proper and right haccording to the New Faith, that is," another cough, "the True Faith. And 'ave wrote the bishops. Fergit 'ow many times we've wrote the bishops. First hoff, they hanswers, *'If any presbyter shall presume to ordain another presbyter, let him be anathema.'* Well, well, seems like sound enough doctrine and no skin hoff my, berumph! Caff caff. But what's it got to do wif dragons? Second time what they replied, *'Satan is the father of lies and the old dragon from the beginning; therefore let no presbyter presume to ordain another presbyter, and if he do presume, let him be anathema.'* " He cast an eye up and around the sky, for all the world like an augur about to take the auspices, then dropped his glance earthwise, and

went on. "Next time we put the question, what's it as
the bishops said, why they said, *'The waters of life
may flow even through the jaws of a dead dog, but if
any presbyter presume to ordain another presbyter—' "*

The gathering murmured, "—*'let him be
anathema.' "*

King Alf then went on, briskly, to inform his
younger guest that from time immemorial, on or
about the hour midway between dawn and high noon
on the third day after the new moon of the month of
Hecatombaeon, a dragon was wont to descend upon
the Land of the Alves for the purpose and with the
intention of carrying off the treasure. *"Dragon?"*
asked Perry, uneasily. "Then why is the treasure out
in the open? And for that matter, why are *we* all out
in the open?" The gathering chuckled.

"Why, bless yer, my boy," the king said,
grinning broadly, "doesn't believe them old tales
about dragons a-living on the flesh of young virgin
females, does yer? Which you be'n't in any event,
leastways I know you be'n't no female, a horhorhor!—No no, see, all them dragons in this zone
and climate o' the world is pie-skiverous, see?
Mayhap and peradventure there be carnivoreal
dragons in the realms of the Boreal Pole; then agin,
mayhap not. No skin hoff my—'O*wever. Yus. Well,
once a year we 'aves this ceremonial rightchual. The
dragon, which 'e's named Smarasderagd (meaning
Lover of Hemeraulds, in th' original Greek), the
dragon comes and tries to carry orf the treasure. *One*
story says, originally twas a golden fleece.
Nowadays, has we no longer lives in thuh world of
my-thology, the treasure is the Treasury. All the
taxes as as been collected under the terms of my

vasselage and doomwit to the 'Igh King, and which I am bound to transmit to 'im—minus seven percent to cover andling expenses—dog licenses, plow orse fee, ox-forge usage, chimbley tax, jus primus noctae commutations in fee simple, and all the rest of it; here he comes now, see 'im skim, thuh hold bugger!''

The crowd cheered, craned their necks, as did Peregrine; sure enough, there was a speck in the sky which rapidly increased in size. Peregrine asked, somewhat perplexed, ''And does the dragon Smarasderagd transmit the treasury to the High King, or—''

King Alf roared, ''What! Fancy such a notion! No no, lad. Old Smarry, 'e makes feint to nobble the brass, yer see, and we drives 'im orf, dontcher see. *I* as to do it hin order to maintain my fief, for, *'Watch and ward agayn Dragons and Gryphons,'* it be written in small print on the bottom of the paytent. And Old Smarry, *'e* as to do it hin order to maintain *'is* rights to hall the trash fish as gits caught in the nets, weirs, seines, wheels, traps and trots hereabouts.—As for gryphons, I don't believe in them things an' nor I shan't, neither, hunless the bishops resolve as I must, hin Council Hassembled. *'Ere* 'e come!''

The spearmen began a rhythmical clashing of their shields.

''Ho serpentine and squamous gurt dragon Smarasderagd,'' the Alf-king began to chant, ''be pleased to spare our treasure . . .''

With a sibilant sound and a strong smell of what Perry assumed was trash fish, the dragon spread his wings into a silent glide and replied, ''I shan't, I shan't, so there and so there and so there . . .''

''Ho serpentine and squamous gurt dragon

Smarasderagd—'ullo, Smarry, 'ow's yer micturating membranes?—be pleased to spare . . .''

"I shan't, I shan't, I shan't—hello, Earwig, mustn't grumble, mustn't grumble—so there and so there and so there . . .''

Clash, clash, clash! went the spearmen. Peregrine observed that their spears had dummy heads.

"Then we'll drive yer away with many wounds and assailments—what's the news, Smarry, is there any news?—assailments and torments . . .''

Swish, swishl, swish, swishl, Smarasderagd flapped his wings and circled low. "That's for me to know and you to find out. My hide is impervious to your weapons, insquamous issue of Deucalion—'' He dug his talons into the sack of treasure, and, on the instant, the spearmen hurled their spears and the slingers whirled their slings and the archers let loose their arrows. And seeing the arrows—which, being made of reeds, and unfletched—bounced harmlessly off Smarasderagd's tough integuments and observing the sling stones to be mere pea gravel, fit for affrighting pigeons, to say nothing of the mock-spears rattling as they ricocheted, Peregrine realized that the resistance was indeed a mere ritually cere-monial one. The dragon in sooth seemed to enjoy it very much, issuing steamy hisses much like giggles as he dug his talons into the sack of treasure and lifted it a space off the ground, while his bright glazey eyes flickered around from face to face and his huge wings beat the air.

Grinning, King Alf said, " 'Ere, 'ave a care now the way yer've got that sack 'eld, Smarry, or ye'll spill it. Don't want us to be a-picken of the Royal Hairlooms, ter say nuffink of the tax drachmae, up from this 'ere muck, do yer?''

"Perish the thought, Earwig," said Smar-asderagd, shifting its grip, and flying higher.

The king's grin slipped a trifle. "Don't play the perishing fool, then," he said. "Settle it back down, smartly and gently."

"I shan't, I shan't, I shan't!"

"What, 'ave yer gotten dotty in yer old age? Set it back down at once directly, does yer 'ear?"

"Screw you, screw you, screw *you*!" And the dragon climbed a bit higher, whilst the king and his subjects looked at each other and at the dragon with a mixture of vexation and perplexity. "I'm not putting it down, I'm taking it with me, a-shish-shish-shish," Smarasderagd snickered steamily.

"But that's again' the rules!" wailed the king.

"It *is* against the rules, isn't it?" the dragon agreed, brightly. "At least, it *was*. But. You know. I've reviewed the entire matter very carefully, and what does it all add up to? To this: you get the treasure and I get the trash fish. So—as you *see*, Earwig—*I've changed the rules!*" He flew a bit higher. "*You* keep the trash fish! *I'll* keep the treasure!"

Buck, who was evidently much quicker than Peregrine had perhaps credited him for, gave a leap and a lunge for the bag of treasure; not only did he miss, but Smarasderagd, with a tittering hiss, climbed higher. Queen Clara, till now silent, tradition having provided no place for her in this pageant save that of spectator, wailed, "Do suthing, Alfland! 'E mustn't get to keep the treasure!"

"I shall, I shall, I shall!" sang out the dragon, and in a slow and majestic manner began to rise.

" 'Ere, now, Smarry," the king implored. "What! Cher going to destroy thur hamicable relations which as 'ithertofore hobtained atween hus for the sake o' this little bit o' treasure which is such in name honely?''

The dragon shrugged—a most interesting sight. "Well, you know how it is," he said. "Here a little, there a little, it all adds up." The king's cry of rage and outrage was almost drowned out by the noise of great rushing as the great wings beat and dragon and treasure alike went up—up—and away. It seemed to Peregrine that, between the sound of the king's wrath and the sound of the beating of the vast ribbed and membranous pinions, he could distinctly hear the dragon utter the words, "Ephtland—Alfland— which will be the next land?''

Needless to say that it was not possible for him then to obtain of this impression either confirmation or refutation.

Having dismissed the Grand Army of Alfland (all nine members of it) and—in broken tones—informed the citizenry that they had his leave to go, King Earwig sat upon an overturned barrel in the middle of his courtyard and, alternately putting his head in his hands and taking it out again, groaned.

"Oh, the hairlooms as come down from King Deucalion's days! Oh, the tax moneys! (Buck, my boy, never trust no reptyle!) Oh . . . What will folk say of me?''

Queen Clara, her normal russet faded to a mere pale pink, had another question to ask, and she asked it. "What will the High King say?''

King Alf-Earwig groaned again. Then he said that he could tell her what the High King would say. " 'Malfeasance, misfeasance, disfeasance, and non-feasance hof hoffice: horf wif is 'ead hon heach count!' is what 'e'll say . . .''

The silence, broken only by the snuffling of
Princess Pearl, was terminated by her mother. "Ah,
and speaking of counts," said she, "what about my
brother-in-law, Count Witenagamote?"

The king's head gave a half flop, and feeling it
as though for reassurance, he muttered, "Ah, and I
spose our only 'opes is ter seek refuge of 'im, for 'e
lives hin a different jurisdiction, 'e does, and holds
not of the High King; holds of the emperor, is what,
the vassal of Caesar 'imself.''

A touch of nature was supplied at this point by
the cock of the yard, who not only ran a slightly
frazzled hen to earth but began to tread her. Buck
barely glanced, so serious was the other situation.
Peregrine asked, automatically, "Which Caesar?"

He asked it of Alf's back, for the king had
gotten up from the barrel and started pacing at
length—a lengthy pace which was now leading him
into the house by the back way. "Which Caesar?"

"Why, bless you," said the king, blankly, "of
Caesar Haugustus, natcherly. What a question. Has
though there were more nor one of 'im.''

Peregrine, who knew very well that there was
not only more than one but that the number of those
using the title of *Caesar*, including heirs, co-heirs,
sovereigns of the East and the West and the Center,
claimants, pretenders, provincial governors and
rather powerful lord mayors and mayors of the
palace, ambitious army commanders—Peregrine,
who knew it would be difficult at any given moment
to calculate how many Caesars there were, also
looked blank, but said nothing. He was clearly very
far from Rome. From any Rome at all.

"Well, well, go we must as we must," muttered

the King. "As we must go we must go. Meanwhile, o'
course," he stopped suddenly, "can't be letting the
Kingdom go wifourt authority; you, there," he
beckoned to the kitchenboy. "How old are you?"

The lad considered, meanwhile wiping his snotty
nose on his apron. "Six, last Mass of the Holy
Martyrs of Macedonia, an' it please Your Worship,"
he piped.

His Worship did some visible arithmetic. "Ah,
that's good," he declared, after a moment. "Then
ye'll not be seven for some munce after the 'Igh
Kingly Hinquisition gits 'ere to check hup . . . as they
will, they will. Below the hage of reason, they can't
do a thing to yer, my boy, beside six smacks hand one
to grow on; so kneel. Hand let's 'ear yer name."

The boy knelt, rather slowly and carefully
placing both palms on his buttocks, and slowly said,
"Vercingetorix Rory Claudius Ulfilas John"—a
name, which, if perhaps longer than he himself was,
gave recognition to most of the cultures which had at
one time or another entered East Brythonia within at
least recorded history.

King Alf tapped him on each shoulder with the
royal dirk without bothering to wipe off the fish
scales (Queen Clara had been cleaning a carp for
supper). "Harise, *Sir* Vercingetorix Rory Claudius
Ulfilas John," he directed. "Not all the way hup,
'aven't finished yet, down we go again. Heh-hem."
He rolled his bulging and bloodshot blue eyes
thoughtfully. "Sir Vercingetorix Rory Claudius
Ulfilas John, we nominates and denominates yer as
Regent *pro tem* of the Kingdoms and Demesnes of
the Lands of the Alfs *in partibus infidelidum*, to have
and to hold from this day forward until relieved by
'Is Royal Highness the 'Igh King—and don't eat all

the raisins in the larder, or he'll have yer hide off yer
bottom, hage of reason or no hage of reason. And
now—'' He looked about. ''Ah, Bert. Yer've been so
quiet, clean forgot yer was present. Ye'll witness this
hact.''

The King of Bertland, simultaneously stiff,
uneasy, unhappy, said, ''That I will, Alf.''

Alf nodded. ''*Hand* now,'' he said, ''let's pack
and hit the pike, then.''

Peregrine had been considering. Amusing
though it might be to tarry and observe how things go
in Alfland under the regency of Sir Vercingetorix
Rory Claudius Ulfilas John (aged six and some), still,
he did not really consider it. And fond though he
already was, though to be sure not precisely deeply
fond—their aquaintance had been too brief—of the
Alvish Royal House, yet he did not really feel that his
destiny required him to share their exile; could he,
even, feel he might depend upon the hospitality of
Count Witenagamote? It might, in fact, be just the
right moment to take his leave . . . before there was
chance for anything more to develop in the way of
taking for granted that he and Princess Pearl—

He was not very keen on dragons. Smarasderagd
was a good deal larger than the last and only previous
dragon he had ever seen. Piscivorous the former
might or might not be; now that he no longer had all
the trash fish to dine upon, who could say? Peregrine
did not feel curious enough to wish to put it to the
test. Dragons might lapse. King Alf's prolegomenal
discourse, just before Smarasderagd had appeared,
seemed to take for granted that the dragon was not a
treasure-amassing dragon; yet all men in Lower
Europe had taken it for granted that all dragons were

by nature and definition just that. Peregrine remembered his first dragon, rather small it had been, and
so—at first glance—had been the treasure it had been
guarding. Yet a further investigation (after the
dragon had been put to flight by the sprig of dragonbane from the geezle-sack of Appledore, the com-
bination sorcerer, astrologer, court philosopher and
a cappella bard of Sapodilla . . . and Peregrine's
boyhood tutor as well . . .) a further, even if ac-
cidental, investigation of the contents of the small
dragon's cave had resulted in Peregrine's—
literally—stumbling upon something of infinitely
more value and weal than the bracelet of base metal
inscribed *Caius loves Mariamne* and the three oboli
and one drachma (all stamped *Sennacherib XXXII,
Great King, King of Kings, King of Lower Upper
Southeast Central Assyria*—and all of a very debased
currency). He had tripped over a rotting leather case
which contained what was believed by the one or two
who, having seen it, were also competent to comment
on it, to be the mysterious and long-lost crown of the
Ephts.

And what *had* Smarasderagd said, as though to
himself, and evidently overheard only by Peregrine
over the noise of the shoutings and the beatings of
leathern wings? It was . . . was it not? . . .
"Ephtland, Alfland, which will be the next land?"

Peregrine said aloud, "It would be a good thing,
in pursuing after him, were we to have with us a sprig
or even a leaf of dragonbane."

King Alf's head snapped back up, his swollen
small eyes surveyed his younger guest from head to
buskin-covered toe. " 'Pursue after 'im,' the lad
says. Ah, me boy, you're the true son of a king,
lawfully hillegitimate though yer be, hand proper fit

for dragon 'unting, too, for, ah, wasn't yer brought back to human form by means hof dragon's hegg?"

Buck's face turned red with pleasure and his teeth shone in his mouth. "That's it, Da!" he exclaimed. "We'll hunt him down, the gurt squamous beasty-thief! And not go running off like—"

Again, though, his mother "had summat to say." And said it. Did Alf think that she and her daughters were going to traipse, like common camp followers, in the train of the Grand Army, whilst he and it went coursing a dragon? ("*Hand* a mad, crack-brain scheme that be, too!") Did Alf, on the other hand, intend that she and her precious daughters should attempt to make their own way to the court of Count Witenagamote, regardless of all perils and dangers along the way, and *unprotected?*

Her husband's reply commenced with a grunt. Then he turned a second time to his older guest, who had been standing first upon one leg and then upon the other. "Bert," he said, "Hi commends me wife and me datters hunto yer mercy, care, and custody, hentreating that ye keeps 'em safe huntil arriving safe at sanctuary, the court of Count Wit. Does yer haccept this charge?"

"*Hac*-cepted!" said the King of Bertland. " 'Ave no fear."

Queen Clara's mouth opened, closed. Before it could open again, the two pettykings were already drawing maps in the sawdust of the kitchen floor with a pair of roasting spits. "Now, Alf, one spot on rowt as yer mussn't homit, is 'ere—" He made a squiggle. " 'Whussat?' Why, that's Place Where The Dragons Dance—"

"Right chew are!" exclaimed King Alf. "For 'e'll be a-prancin' 'is trihumph there for sure (Buck, my boy, never trust no reptyle).''

"Likewise," King Bert warmed to the matter, "don't forget 'e'll 'ave to be returning *'ither*," he made another scrawl, "to is aerie-nest at Ormesthorpe, for 'e've a clutch o' new-laid heggs—"

Peregrine, puzzled, repeated, with altered accent, "He's got a clutch of—*what*?"

"Come, come, young man," said King Bert, a trifle testily, "Hi 'asn't the time ter be givin' yer lessons hin nat'ral 'istory: suffice ter say that hall pie-skiverous dragons his hambisextuous, the darty beasts!''

Something flashed in Peregrine's mind, and he laid his hand upon King Bert's shoulder. "It seems destined that I be a party to this quest for the Treasury carried off by gurt dragon Smarasderagd," he said, slowly. "And . . . as King Alf has pointed out, it was a dragon's egg that helped restore me to human form . . . a dragon's egg which, I have been informed, is now in your own and rightful custody: now therefore, O King of Bertland, I, Peregrine, youngest son of the left hand of Paladrine King of Sapodilla, do solemnly entreat of you your kindness and favor in lending me the aforesaid dragon's egg for the duration of the aforesaid quest; how about it?''

Sundry expression's rippled over King Bert's craggy face. He was evidently pleased by the ceremonial manner of the request. He was evidently not so pleased about the nature of it. He swallowed. "What? . . . Wants the mimworms, too, does yer? . . . Mmmm.''

"No, no. Just the egg, and purely for purposes of matching it with any other eggs as I might be finding; a pretty fool I'd look, wouldn't I, were I to waste time standing watch and ward over some nest or other merely because it had eggs in it—and then have them turn out to be, say, a bustard's . . . or a crocodile's . . ."

This argument was so persuasive to the other king that he even, as he unwrapped the object from its wad of scarlet-dyed tow, bethought himself of other reasons—" 'Like cleaves hunto like,' has Harisdottle says, may it bring yer hall good luck, ar, be sure as it will"—and rewrapping it, placed it in his very own privy pouch. He then had Peregrine remove his own tunic, slung pouch and contents so that it hung under the left (or shield) arm. "There. Cover hup, now, lad," he said.

Matters suddenly began to move more rapidly after that, as though it had suddenly occurred to everyone that they didn't have forever. Provisions were hastily packed, arms quickly and grimly sorted and selected. The Grand Army of the Alves was also remustered, and four of its nine members found fit for active duty in the field. Of these, however, one—a young spearman—was exempted because of his being in the first month of his first marriage; and a second, an archer, proved to have a painful felon or whitlow on his arrow thumb. This left one other archer, a short bowman whose slight stature and swart complexion declared more than a drop or two of autochthonous blood, and a very slightly feeble-minded staff slinger, said to be quite capable of doubling as spearman in close-in fighting. ("Moreover 'e's the wust poacher in the kingdom and so should damn well be able to spot dragon spoor—d'ye hear, ye clod?" "Har har! Yus, Mighty Monarch.")

The procession was obliged to pause moment-
arily in the open space before the cathedral church
(indeed, the only church), where the Mitred Protopresbyter and Apostolic Vicar (in which capacity
he held episcopal orders to ordain presbyters) had
suddenly become very visible. As usual, he had
absented himself from the dragon ceremony on the
ground of dragons being essentially pagan creatures
which had not received the approbation of any
church council; he was uncertain if he should pronounce a ritual gloat at the dragon's having been the
cause of the king's discomfiture, or if he should give
the king the church's blessing for being about to go
and hunt the heathen thing; and he had summoned
his catechumens, doorkeepers, deacons, subdeacons,
acolytes and excorcists to help him in whichever task
he hoped right now to be moved by the Spirit to
decide.

A small boy who had climbed the immemorial
elm abaft the cathedral church to get a good view,
suddenly skinnied down and came running. Peregrine's was the first face he encountered and
recognized as being noteworthy; so, "Eh, Meyster!"
he exclaimed. "There come three men on great
orses towards th' Eastern Gate, and one on 'em
bears a pennon with a mailed fist—"

King Alf whirled around. *"Kyrie eleison!"* he
exclaimed. " 'Tis Baron Bruno, the High King's
brutal brother-in-law and *ex officio* Guardian of the
Gunny Sacks (Treasury Division). What brings him
here so untimely? He'll slay me, he'll flay me—"

Peregrine said, "Take the Western Gate. See
you soonly," and gave the King's mount a hearty
slap on the rump. The clatter of its hooves still in his
ears, he strode up to the ecclesiast on the church

steps, the Vicar Apostolic regarding him so sternly
that one might almost have thought he was able to
discern that the waters of baptism had never yet been
sprinkled, poured, or ladled upon Peregrine's still-
pagan skin.

"Your Apostolic Grace," Peregrine asked, in
urgent tones, "it is surely not true—*is* it?—that one
presbyter may ordain another presbyter?"

The hierarch beat the brazen butt of his crosier
on the church step with such vehemence that the
catechumens, doorkeepers, deacons, subdeacons,
acolytes and exorcists came a-running.

"It *is* false!" he cried, in a stentorian voice.
"Cursed be who declares the contrary! Where is he,
the heretic dog?"

Peregrine gestured. "Coming through the
Eastern Gate even now," he said. "And one of them
bears the pennon of a mailed fist, alleged to be the
very sign and symbol of presbytocentrism!"

The apostolic vicar placed two fingers in his
mouth, gave a piercing whistle, hoisted his crosier
with the other, beckoned those in minor orders—and
in none—"All hands fall to to repel heretics!" he
bellowed. He had long formerly been chaplain with
the Imperial Fleet. The throng, swelling on all sides,
poured after him towards the Eastern Gate.

Peregrine mounted the shag Brythonic cob
which had been assigned him, smote its flanks,
whooped in its ears, and passed out through the
Western Gate with deliberate speed. The dragon egg
nestled safe beneath his arm.

*Hours and days and months and years go by;
the past returns no more, and what is to be we
cannot know; but whatever the time gives us in
which to live, we should therefore be content.*
—*CICERO [or maybe Horace]*

The Emperor of the East was also perplexed: whereas hithertofore all had been relatively simple—either he supported the Greens' teams in the chariot races, who were Orthodox, or else he supported the Blues' teams in the chariot races, who were Monophosytes (or perhaps it was the other way around): in either case, of course, risking riot, rebellion, and the loss of both Diadem and Purple (and perhaps also of both his eyes)—*now* he was suddenly being faced with other and even less welcome alternatives: the Reds, who were either Donatists or Arians; the Whites, who vehemently advanced the claims of the Nestorians—and the Emperor of the East at that instant could not tell the difference between the Arians and the Nestorians to save his *life*

("Know a good *horse*, when I see one, though," he used to say, wistfully)—or was it the Montanists?—and, all so suddenly (and, it seemed to him, so unfairly); the Beiges and the Mauves, whose religious choices . . . couldn't all of them have simply *raced chariots?* . . . No they *could*n't! . . . were even more *outré* . . . consisting of the United Gnostic Front, which included Basilideans, Valentinians, Marcionites, and Manichaeans; and the Eikonoklasts, who were particularly down on anyone who spelled their name as "Iconoclasts."

The immediate problems of the Emperor of the West were perhaps less complex. *He* was, in a way, chiefly concerned with budgetary problems. Should he pay a sweetener of a hundred thousand pounds of gold to the Vandals, who threatened, otherwise, to sack Rome again, after having once sacked it in such a manner as to leave their name as a word forever horrid in the language . . . ?

Or should he pay a retainer, a gift, so-called, of a hundred thousand pounds of gold to the Ostrogoths, who were growing very, *very* restive, with their backs to the Alps, and in daily fear of cold drafts and of avalanches . . . ?

These choices, equally unsatisfactory, were further complicated by the circumstances that his Treasury contained barely thirty thousand pounds in gold altogether: and had upon it constant other claims, ranging from the repairs of the aqueducts (which leaked so incessantly that poets used the fact as a given) to the payment of the arrears of the standing army: for the days were past when legions received a salary sufficient only to buy salt.

On the whole he inclined to think that he would give one-third of it to the soldiery, lest they desert him sooner than later; use one-third to pay for a nice marble tomb with lavish inscriptions . . . *And Conqueror of the Vandals and the Ostrogoths*, for example;—one could say what one liked on inscriptions, as for the most part of course the Barbarians could not read;—and allocate the final one-third to the Pope (in those days Rome had its own Pope) for requiem masses; The Emperor of the West was anyway doomed, and full well he knew it.

As for the Emperor of the Midst . . . Ambrosius Lucianus had there and then most recently been proclaimed; and he had followed the distribution of the customary donations (from the Captains of the Guards down to the Inspectors of Water Mains and Sewer Drains) with the pronouncement of a doctrine the most bizarre of which anyone had, anywhere, at any time, ever heard, *videlicet, Complete Freedom of Religion*. This new policy was bound to bring peace to the Central Roman Empire. Only maybe not. Pagan and Neo-Pagan, Jew and Christian and Heretic (Gnostic, Agnostic, or otherwise) paused in The Bath and Forum and Agora and looked at each other, baffled. "Either I am right or you are right or you are right or *you* are right: this is obvious. And whosoever is right (although this is of course mere rhetoric, for of course *I* am right!) is he who holds the truth; and it is the most commonplace bit of logic in the *world*, which every child can understand and even he who runs may read, that Truth owes no tolerance to Error . . ."

But there were of course those who cared for none of these things and who simply came briskly into their offices, sat down briskly at their desks, briskly unrolled their maps and said to their associates and their subordinates, "Now here is

where the ancient sacrifices have been suppressed and
here is where they are now tō be revived, for the good
of the State, the good of the Imperium, for Piety and
Patriotism, and all the rest of it: you see: Here. And
here. And *here*.''

Briskly.

As the troops and court and camp followers of
the High King of East Brythonia came clumping in
through the Nigh, or Eastern Gate of Alfland High
Town, Peregrine was making with all deliberate haste
out of Alftown via the Aft, or Western Gate.

He had, he thought, set up sufficient diversion
to cover the escape of himself and his friends, but to
have remained and checked on the success of his
stratagem would have defeated the whole purpose of
it. Either the Mitred Vicar Apostolic of Alvish East
Brythonia, and his pious parishioners, believing (as
Peregrine had intended they should) that the in-
comers were indeed a group of schismatic Arians
holding the diabolical doctrine of anti-mitre, that
One presbyter may ordain another presbyter, would
subdue and send them flying back the way they came,
thus permitting King Alf of the Alves and his handful
of followers time to make a clean get-away, or . . . or
he would not. And *they* would not.

In which case—

But Peregrine preferred not to dwell upon in
which case.

Up ahead he heard, or thought he heard, the
sounds of the hoofbeats of his friends now flying,
and resisted an urge to spur on his horse. For one
thing, his horse was no Pegasus, but a slow and
heavy beast which only earlier that morning had been
engaged in plowing the parsnip field in the royal

south forty, and one unused to being spurred. He was, to be sure, encouraged by his rider's knees, moving at somewhat more than plow-speed, but his rider had a notion that, were his (the horse's) flanks to be rowelled with spurs, he (the horse) might simply stop moving altogether.

In which case—

Furthermore, it was not immediate speed or even deliberate haste which was the first desideratum: endurance was that. And *further*more—

Furthermore, Peregrine, pleased with his own remorseless logic, now all at once realized that he *had* no spurs. None whatsoever. Not even one.

So he contented himself with saying, from time to time, as he dug his knees in, "Get thee up!" (or, as the local dialect had it, "Git dee ap!"—and, when this failed, as it oftimes did, even to keep the pace, with murmurs of, "*Nice* horsey . . . *Nice* horsey . . .")

Thus engaged, he failed to observe that the wheel-, foot-and-hoof-prints now ahead belonged chiefly to the Town Water Cart and its carter, who had passed very early that morning on their way to Alf Pond, and that for the most part, all the most recent prints had diverged onto a largely grassgrown and weeny side-road, not much better than a path. Someone in the Royal Entourage had of a sudden recollected this as an old short-cut and no one in the Royal Entourage had recollected that Peregrine, having never passed this way in his life before, had no way of recollecting it as such (or as anything else) at all. No one even thought to pause and leave for him a signal such as a broken branch or a line of pebbles.

No one even thought of anything . . . except, of course, escape.

Escape from the High King who would, upon learning (as almost at once he would) that the Treasure (including the Taxes) had been stolen by a dragon . . . by *any* dragon . . . or by any other means . . . would at once begin to demonstrate that the only thing which distinguished his own lack of grace under pressure from that of the nastier Roman Emperors was that his own cruelties and excesses had of necessity to be on a much narrower scale, by his own choice to be much less expensive . . .

. . . and, of course, by his own absolute lack of class or style.

No one would be dipped in tar and burnt alive: tar was expensive, and was reserved for use in the High Royal Roof-mending Monopoly. No one would be fed to maddened lions: lions were *dam*nably expensive, maddened or otherwise. But anybody might of course be impaled, for the cost of a sharpened pole was minimal; and anybody of course might be plonked into a dungeon and there left to starve to death: which cost, of course, and therein lay its beauty, *nothing at all!*

Hence the haste of King Alf. And all the rest of them.

The skill in spooring possessed by the wise Athenian mentioned in the Talmud (and also under many other names in many other sources, thus proving how widely the Talmud has been read and by how many people who know a good story when they see it)—the one who was able at a glance to adduce that there had passed along the way a she-camel such-and-such-a-number of months great with colt, blind in one eye, and carrying oil in one pack and we forget exactly what in the other—this skill was not Peregrine's.

He followed the road.

And, lined with oak and beech and sorb-apple and sorb-plum and hedge and thicket and bush and brush, it was, with all its wendings and its windings, a very long, long road indeed.

It was not any common thing for any petty king to avoid the annual Visitation of and set meeting with his overlord and high king; it was not common, no. It was, however, not unknown. It was, however, unknown for such a reason, *videlicet*, that the petty king's carelessness had allowed a dragon to steal the treasury. But, although no dragon had ever before stolen a treasury, still, a treasury had been stolen before. The High King of East Brythonia could not, certainly, excuse such conduct: on the part of the dragon, it constituted malfeasance, and on the part of the petty king of the Alves, it constituted misfeasance.

Therefore, that the misfeasant king should have gone to chase after the malfeasant dragon was easy to understand. And did this king return with the money, be sure that sundry many fines and other penalties would be levied upon—and collected . . . *and collected*—from him, be sure. But there was more to this than the High King could easily comprehend.

And the "more" in this case was . . . Peregrine . . .

"Afore they cut an' run," demanded His Highness, " 'oo'd been 'ere?" The question was all but *pro forma*, but Bryon of Brythonia (East) cared not to take chances. And it cost nought to ask. Answer was, if not entirely satisfactory, swift. The King of the Alves, his Queen, the two princesses, the one prince, and the one other petty king, evidently not involved in the matter of the missing treasure (though of course, as his turn for the Visitation had not yet come, come it would), and, also, one other guest. The High King supposed, with heavy, scornful sarcasm, no more: *Another* king?

Well . . . no . . . not another king. But the son of another king.

At once High King Bryon's large, hairy, dirty ears pricked up.

Son of a *what*? Of *what* king and *which* king?—this could not be clearly learned. Now the High King knew where each and every petty king and the heirs of same, in East Brythonia, were at the moment . . . or were supposed at the moment to be . . . for none of them might by law leave their realms without notice being given, with reason, purpose, and destination . . . and he could bring to mind no son of a king, and certainly of no such description, who was intended to be present in Alfland. He could rack his brain in vain for any who might even be suspected of being present.

"Peregrine . . . a son of a king . . . young . . . slender . . . dark and comely . . ."

"Peregrine," son of a king, and of a king unknown? It was all puzzling, baffling, mystifying.

And so, of course, dangerous. Very, very dangerous.

Bryon had growled, had shouted, had asked questions, had sought suggestions: all in vain. No further information was forthcoming . . . save one small bit, supplied by one of those whom it would be flattery indeed to term a delator, or even an informer: one of those who always have at least one something to say (and, if afterwards, faced with having said something, demand, "What did I say? I said nothing! All I said was," and so on) if for no better reason than to be heard saying something . . . and to be listened to whilst saying it . . .

" 'E wore a green tunical, and trews wi' a great brown check h'a-woven h'inter 'um, may it save Your 'Ighness.''

"Much that tells me," growled Bryon High King. For a moment more he sat grumbling and casting his eyes low about the cluttered mucky courtyard, then his eyes and he himself all together rose.

He looked—he glared, rather—at the Lord Grumpit, Baron Bruno, his brother-in-law (the sister and wife who united them in whatsoever law it was, not regarded by either, was not part of the procession; she was back home plucking geese, quite content that neither of the main men in her life was paying her attentions, for little, and, in fact, no pleasures had she ever got from the attentions of —the Baron was his Next-at-Arms—

—But here an interpolation: whilst the High King's men had come sloping and slouching into Alftown, expecting no more than the usual boredom mitigated merely by brief rest and country fare and fornication in way of refreshment, the Baron himself riding before his men and casting his eyes all round with less lack of lustre than most (for he suspected everything, everywhere, anyplace, anytime), he saw passing along on a lumbering horse at the far end of a leafy lane a younger man than he by far. The Baron could read letter in no language (he could identify the CHI RHO but it is doubtful he recognized them as letters; it is doubtful that he kenned but little more about them than that they were a sign of power . . . and of what power or Power he scarcely kenned at all) but the Baron's eyes were keener than any man's.

And his ears, sharper.

Almost at the same time as he saw the younger man he heard a girl, one in early womanhood, say, "There he goes! That is him!" and the mere tone of her voice did bad things to him, for no woman of any stage of womanhood had ever spoken to, or, he was sure, and rightly sure, of he himself in such a tone. And another voice, young and fresh and clear (he saw neither of these girls, they were hid from him by trees; perhaps (he thought now) he would when chance availed go thither and see could he find either one of them, and make her say . . . well, it mattered not what she would say) the other young girl's voice said one word.

"*Peregrine* . . ."

And the Baron had marked in the one instant that the figure who swiftly entered and swiftly left his line of sight at the end of the long and leafy lane was young . . . slender . . . dark and comely . . . and clad in a green tunical, and in trews with a great brown check woven into them. Somehow, he did not (in what he had in place of what most men had for minds) at the moment realize everything he saw, heard, felt: not all in that one moment. But . . . Now . . .

And now the High King Bryon glared at him, and said, sunken mouth twitching, "Take five men. Go. Follow." The orders of the said High King to him were commonly succinct; for one thing, in matters purely (or impurely) military he knew . . . and loved it not . . . that the Baron Bruno had the better skill; thus, did the Baron in despite of scant orders do well, he had but obeyed and so earned no praise; for another, did the Baron in despite of scant orders do ill, then Bryon could not blame himself.

No one else, of course, could blame Bryon.

Not openly.

Who now added almost before he had finished his first words, "What! You are still 'ere? *Harms! Orse! Presue! Fetch! Begorn!*"

The Baron lowered his heavy eyes, set his heavy jaws still more heavily together, looked round for five good (which is to say, bad) men, beckoned with his mailed fist. In his hoarse voice he said, after as brief a formal obeisance as he dared, "*March!*"

The hornsman sounded something inarticulate. The two horsemen clattered forward but—carefully—not too far forward—the foot clumped behind, dragging their pikes, yawning, cursing low, spitting and farting and scratching their armpits; all casting sidelong looks when they passed any woman (or even boy) rash enough to be still abroad.

For the King of Alfland, the Baron felt about as much as he felt for the roach which scuttles away across the floor: a certain desire to crush it: no more. But slowly now for Peregrine he the Baron had been developing a different feeling altogether. For Peregrine was young and the Baron had once been young but Peregrine was also comely and also admired and the Baron had never been comely and never at any hour had he ever been admired. Some to be sure did envy him. But of all shadows of admiration, envy is the least. And . . . it was said . . . Peregrine was the son of a king, though of which king it was not said: of none he had ever known, the Baron was sure. *A king!* The Baron was no king's son, though supposedly, he was *some* man's son . . .

Of the Emperor and the Emperor's glory, the Baron had heard, in much the same manner he had heard of the God and the God's glory: and now and then he thought, with some sullen wonder, of either

the One or the other. Some day he might see the God.
Some day he might see the Emperor. But from one
day to the next, unless some other mentioned either,
the Baron thought not at all of either the God or of
the Emperor.

He did, however, think about the king. About
the High King. The Baron was at all times incapable
of putting himself in another's place, save of course
that he was at all times capable of putting himself in
the High King's place and he knew what *he* would do
if *he* were high king and this other one—the Baron
Bruno—did dare make one, *one*, move for the
throne, and so knowing this he did not dare make
that one move—

Among the High King's subjects were many who
would have dared move, not to take for themselves
the throne, the high throne, but to help those who
might help remove from that throne the man who
squatted on it like a mangy wolf, but who did not,
would not, make such a one move, because they
knew that while the Baron lived the throne was
potentially the Baron's if ever the High King left it or
was at all weakened whilst yet upon it. Gold, they
knew, would stay the High King. But it was in their
minds and hearts that nothing at all would stay the
Baron.

And this was the man who now followed after
Peregrine.

The High King at length, and followed by his
followers, sallied out of Alf Big House to show his
power, and to see who'd bow—actually, of course,
he had no thought but what *every*body would bow; it
was his intention, first, to catch up with all

profugitives, and, second, to sack the place for all it
was worth—"followed," that is, by all but one of his
followers. It was his practice invariable to send his
Grand Chaplain riding ahead, in case, just in case,
there should be in the road any caltraps, cantrips,
man-traps, dead-falls, covered pits, or pagan curses.
This function was, in His Highness's opinion, one of
the chief functions of a Grand Chaplain. If not the
chief*most*. The chaplain did not by any means agree.
But he had long since learned to accept the task with
a truly Christian forbearance.

And an occasion to pray with very great sin-
cerity.

Thus it was that the Grand Army of East
Brythonia, its High King and High Court, came
marching *south* along the Paved Street at the same
time as the Mitred (and, perhaps, who knows, and
who knew how soon? martyred) Protopresbyter and
Apostolic Vicar of Alvish East Brythonia, his cure
and flock, came marching *north*. Now: had Baron
Bruno, the High King's brother-in-law and *ex officio*
C. in C., been the first in his line of march, short
work would have been made of any and all who did
not instanta fling themselves face downward crying
the good old (and, but one must whisper this)
originally Pagan cry of "O High King, live forever!"
(doctrinally dubious, of course, else the entire study
of eschatology may go for nought)—but protocol, to
say nothing of the High King, forbade such precedence. Also: had the Mitred Protopresbyter's right-
hand man, in private life a short-tempered boss
butcher, been first in *his* line of march—

However.

Grand Chaplain and Mitred Protopresbyter (an
office combined in the Arian Church with that of

Apostolic Vicar wherever qualified prelates were in
short supply) at once recognized each other as a
member of an opposite side at many and many a
Church Council: they had exchanged words at the
Council of Cappadocia, they had split hairs at the
Council of Boeotia, they had—for once, and only for
once—joined at the Council of Babylonia Philadelphia in flinging *cathedrae* at those putting forth
the damnable doctrine of Justification by Good
Works, i.e., Works of Corporal Mercy. Local loyal-
ties at once went for nothing, and present politics for
less than nothing.

The Grand Chaplain dismounted from his mule
and—though only on one knee—genuflected before
the   Mitred Protopresbyter. The Mitred Protopresbyter lifted his mitre with both hands—though
only one inch—and, replacing it, aspersed the Grand
Chaplain. The niceties had been observed.

"Clement of Alexandria," began the Grand
Chaplain.

"Theophilus of Antioch," began the Mitred
Protopresbyter (and Vicar Apostolic).

Everyone relaxed. It might all end in bloodshed
yet. But yet was not yet. There was, after all,
nothing, *nothing*, like a nice, good long theological
argument. The local throng now offered the invaders
first fruits and other fresh produce. The soldiery offered the citizenry salt pickles and crisp biscuits.
Even the High King, though he bit his long and filthy
nails and growled a bit, even he accepted a sliced cold
melon from the local fruit-merchant, and cocked his
rather dirty ear to the sacred discourse.

"Perpetual damnation without preamble or
Purgatory," from one of the archpriests.

"Occasional and intermittent respite and refreshment, by Grace, of those in torment,'' from one of the others.

The High King slurped his sliced cold melon; when it was gone he reached out for another. The missing Treasure might be somewhere and then again it might be somewhere else: where it was, was not certain. The missing petty king and petty court might be making good their escape; then again they might not be making good their escape: what they might be doing was not certain.

"And it is written, 'Where their worm dieth not, and their fire is not quenched'—"

"And where is it written, 'But their worm never dieth, and their fire is never quenched'?''

Only one thing, after all, was absolutely certain, let this rabble and any other rabble shout their *Live forevers* till their throats went dry, only one thing was utterly certain. *All men are mortal.*

All men must die.

The High King sate upon his horse. And he listened. And he stayed.

After what seemed a very long time, Peregrine had to concede that he heard nothing whatsoever ahead of him anymore: no tlot-tlot, no tramp-tramp, no murmurs of hush, no inadvertent sounds such as all but the most disciplined of troop must e'en sometimes make, not even a whinny or a neigh.

He halted his horse.

The horse at once moved over to the barm of the road and began to graze.

All was silent.

And, still, Peregrine heard nothing.

Some scent, he though it must be, some scent remembered from early childhood, honeysuckle perhaps, or hawthorne or acacia, overwhelmed him, and, mixed with so many other childhood sensual reflections—the smell of the rank weed and grass crushed by the horse's hooves—and, indeed, the smell of the horse itself, *don't thee be afeared now Perry for Dada has ahold o' thee*, and the very feel of the animal between his legs (for most of the trip so far he'd had little time to allow for reflections on such like) . . . and other sounds and such from childhood began to rise up on all sides, as the humming of sundry insects and the buzzing of bees, Nnn-nnnnnn . . . Whshshshhh . . . the very leaves of the trees began to whisper to him, as in days of old, as in former years . . . Perry Perry listen listen: so the sounds seemed to say . . . hadn't, in his childhood, when all was fresh, all innocent, all there for him, hadn't sound in the seas of trees seemed to say that to him? Yes they had. And what else had they seemed to say?

He let himself be swept away by Memory, sweet sister, or was it sweet daughter of . . . perry perry listen listen listen perry child go not upon this road much further and neither turn back the way of coming, for—

What?

He had no childhood memory of *these* words at all.

Not at *all*.

But, and in but a second more, he realized: it was *now* that he was hearing this! In his childhood, indeed he had heard the voices in the woods speaking to him, with their *Perry, Perry, listen, Perry*. But then they had said other things to him, and what they had said to him then was one thing, and what they were saying now was another. Quite another. "I hear you and I am listening," he said now. Aloud, yes. But not very loud. It was not necessary to speak very loud.

Not to the dryads, who spoke to him now from every shrub and tree.

From almost every . . .

A deeper hum and thrum and rustle now took up the theme and he recognized this one, too. The Man in the Oak . . .

"Peregrine, we speak to thee and thou canst hear us, for we perceive that thine ears have not been estopped against our voices; there is that sheen about thee which sheweth us that the waters have not been cast upon thee, that thou hast not been immersed in those waters which close the ears of man and child and woman against us forever."

And he, Peregrine, acknowledged that it was true. "I am a heathen still," he said. "A child of the wild heath. And I hear you and I listen."

The dryads repeated their soft, sweet murmur. *"Listen, listen, listen, Perry, child, go not upon this road much further and neither turn back the way of coming, for there is danger ahead as there is danger behind . . ."*

And the bees made their solemn oath and affirmation, with their solemn sound and note of *Nnn-nnnnnnn . . .*

"I have listened and I have heard and I have believed and do believe you," he said. "What, then, am I to—"

The dryads, half-saying, half-singing: *"We shall ask our bigger brother . . ."*

The Man in the Oak, with his deeper thrum and hum and rustle, made reply: *"And I shall ask mine elder brother . . ."*

From an even more immense tree now came an even deeper, droning voice. "*Sister Dryads, Brother Oak, Peregrine* parens, *I am thy Brother Beech, who, being asked, must answer. Peregrine: long ago, how long ago I cannot say, but many snows and many springs ago it was, and many wolves have whelped, and it may be even that I saw the oliphant beneath my boughs, who has gone, ah long has the oliphant gone from beneath my boughs from one horizon to the other; but I grow prolix; I must be brief: on a day long, long ago came men and cut my sister down—*" The dryads keened and sobbed a moment; then their sound became subdued; the beach tree, towering high above them all, resumed: "*—and cut my sister down, and of her substance many things they made, the usages of which I wot not for the most part: but this I know: of her heart they made certain boards and worked them smooth—for this was before even the days when men made tablets and inlaid them with wax—and on these boards, Peregrine my kith (for thou wast begotten beneath a beechen tree, didst thou this know? it matters not, but—), upon these boards made of my Sister Beech—*"

And, suddenly, there burst upon Peregrine's mind and burst from out his lips, words which he had heard before, and had wondered on, and had then—till now—forgotten:

"'*Beware the boards of beechwood with the baleful signs!*'"

And all the trees then swayed, and every bough bowed *Yes*.

And every bough bowed *Yes*.

Ambrosius Lucianus having assumed the Diadem and Purple (and with them also the traditional names of Augustus Hadrian Nerva Constans Maximin Trajan, and so on and SO on . . . ''Caesar' being understood,) had issued as one of his first edicts that all religious ceremonies were legal, whatsoever—save those involving human sacrifice and human male castration—and at once ceased to be known by most of those nobly assumed names. Christians called him Ambrose the Apostate, and pagans referred to him as Lucian the Liberator. And, among the many, *many* results of his edict and decree was that once again lots were to be drawn to select the members of the College of Priests to officiate at the ever-so-ancient Iguvine Games. These were not really and had not for donkeys' ages actually been games in any but the most archaically dubious sense of the word; in fact, they were not actually being performed in Iguvium proper at all, for Iguvium proper lay in Umbria proper, and this was still within the domain and dominion of the Emperor of the West, but *New* Iguvium (with which we are concerned) lay in *New* Umbria, and *New* Umbria was an ancient old Umbrian colony which had from ancient times offered its annual sacrifices according to the ancient Umbrian customs, said customs requiring the presence of a two-man college of priests. The college had once been larger, *lots* larger, but, as ancient although of course still at least semi-sacred languages such as Etruscan, Oscan, Umbrian, Lydian, Lybian, AEgyptian (Orthodox and Reformed), and others, had tended to drop from the curriculum year by sad year, to be replaced by the new-fangled trivium and quadrivium; so the number of potential candidates had dropped as well.

Such priests had of course to be of noble blood and of the aristocracy (true, the once razor-sharp

lines dividing Patricians from Knights was now a
thing of the past . . . particularly in the Central or
Middle Roman Empire), they had each to possess all
four limbs and all twenty digits (the nice point, would
one be eligible who had more than twenty digits?
Had never ever been settled; and, almost certainly, now
never would be), and one penis and two
testicles—each; between them would not do—and
they, of course, had, of course, to be able to perform
the ceremony in *Umbrian*. Umbrian, like Oscan, was
an Italic tongue akin to Latin, but it *was not*
Latin . . .

. . . and it was almost extinct.

In fact: it was doubtful if there were now as
many as six or seven otherwise eligible candidates
who could count up to five in Umbrian, even upon
their fingers. However, the decree had gone forth
that the ceremonies were to be performed and the
sacrifices to be held, and so five eligible and elderly
knights had turned out to draw lots to see which two
would go and hold them.

They were to be known, according to the old law
and custom, as the Aetidian Brothers: and the elder
was to be the Brother-Superior.—*or*, if one preferred, the Elder Brother.

Free snacks were always available on the occasion of such selections, there was of course the
privilege of serving the immortal gods (rather, of
late, having been rather neglected; at any rate, certainly, having been rather officially neglected), there
was of course the honor of the thing, and there was,
in addition, the official perquisites, consisting of a
bushel of golden emmerrods, a peck of gold mice,
three gold rings and a silver tassy apiece . . . and sun-

dry other items, all of a most valuable and a most eclectic nature.

This was not indeed the first time in recent years that the lots had been drawn, but this was the first time they had been drawn openly for some time. And the first time in all that time that they had been drawn with any much expectation that the twain chosen would be allowed actually to travel to Nova Umbria openly and in expectation of actually holding and performing the ceremonies. However. One of the five candidates was quite obviously senile and kept wiping his nose upon his *toga prætexta*, one had had to be carried to the comitium, or polling place in his potty-chair—he was still mentally alert enough but his physical infirmity *did* raise questions—one, and, alas, the youngest one, was well-known to be given to seizures of the sacred sickness ("Same as Great Caesar himself, and what of it?" demanded the aggressive—(some added, greedy)—great-nephew who accompanied him: but well did he and everyone else know what of it: should an attack of the sacred, or, as it was also called, the falling, sickness, occur . . . occur at any official gathering . . . it was taken as evidence the most obvious that some god was present . . . and, for whatsoever reasons, desired to interrupt; and even the Senate itself was automatically adjourned at such times) and so . . .

And so there were *two*.

Now, new religions, in newly civilized regions, might find insoluble the problems of five people drawing lots for an exercise of which only two were patently capable, but the lands round about the Tideless and Innermost and Circumfluent Seas were too old and too sophisticated for that: an experienced præstidigitator always held the lot-box. When one of the undesired candidates dipped his hand, the conjuror simply and deftly slipped him a black ball.

The returns were , not unexpectedly, as desired. Or, anyway, as desired by those in charge. Which is, in the long run, the same thing.

And so there, amidst the marble columns and between the marble walls (concrete, actually, but very skillfully veneered with marble), "Chosen thereby to serve the immortal gods in the capacity of Brothers of the Aetidian College of Priests at the Gubbian Games in New Gubbio," ancounced the selectoral officer, in a mixture of the new idiom and the old, "are the Right Honorable Senator Sir Rufus Tiburnus, Pat., Kt., Senatus Publiusque Romanum Proconsul (Ret.) . . . *and*" . . . he made a feint of consulting his tablets . . . "the Right Honorable Senator Sir Zosimus Sulla, Pat., Kt., Senatusconsultum de Bacchanalibus (Ret.)." Here he hesitated. *Was* there supposed to be a ritual mumble of *absit omen* at this point?—or was there *not* suppose to be a ritual murmur of *absit omen* at this point? He gazed, in some perplexity, at a bust of the Divine Guphus, a deservedly obscure Emperor, which had only recently been taken out of storage and placed in an empty niche for lack of anything else then and there immediately available. . . . Were they all waiting for him to indicate . . . ? Or were they *not* all waiting for him to indicate? Being one of the rare officials who had risen to office by tact rather than treachery, he solved the matter very admirably: he sneezed. Everybody at once mumbled *absit omen* . . . except for one newly naturalized citizen and new-made knight, a former petty king from out the Gothic North or East, who mumbled something which sounded like *gezundtheit*, but which of course was not.

". . . may the gods send thee good victims and auspicious signs," the official continued smoothly, running through the rest of the general formulae; then, coming to what someone (perhaps one of the two selected) was heard to refer to, not too *sotto voce*, as *the point*: "Both litters and carriages will be provided, and change of horses and/or mules at all Imperial posting-stops, plus daily allowances for the bating and victualling of their beasts, plus that for the servants, whether free-born or freed, or slave, serf or thrall, *and*," and here he cleared his throat and raised his voice and looked around him with an air of one who has wrought well and deserved well, "and all this and the maintenance of the Collegiate Priests *pro temporae et pro hac vice* shall be equal to that of those of the rank of Caesar, both coming and returning, *salve adque vale*, the Rev. Sir Rufus Tiburnus and *salve adque vale*, the Rev. Sir Zosimus Sulla . . . the wine . . . the water . . . the libations . . . the refreshments . . . and the free souvenirs for the august candidates who were on this occasion not selected to be chosen by the immortal gods . . ."

"Not bad arrangements, what?" said the Rev. Sir Zosimus Sulla to the Rev. Sir Rufus Tiburnus. ("Reverend," of course, was brevet-rank.)

"Not bad arrangements at all, you know," said Sir Rufus Tiburnus to Sir Zosimus Sulla. "Must go home and pack me bags; get an early start, what?"

"Yes, yes. Get a very early start. And let us both be sure to dress up very warm, remember poor old Ovid, chap absolutely perished with the cold. And . . . ah . . . and . . ."

"Yes? What else had you in mind?"

"Well, tell you the truth, not *sure*. What I had in mind. Hm. *Oh*. Trifling matter, to be sure. *Still*. In view of, ah, sundry possibilities? Religious unrest? Barbarian incursions?"

Sir Rufus was becoming just a bit restless. "What do you mean, 'religious unrest'? Decree has gone forth from Caesar Augustus, hasn't it? Chaps can follow any religion they want, can't they? As for 'Barbarian incursions,' stuff and nonsense; barbarians were defeated at the last annual incursion and sent home with the usual rich gifts. Won't be another incursion till . . . till . . . well, the actual date hasn't actually been decided on—very late next Spring, I should expect. *Af*ter the freshets."

Sir Zosimus took a moment to digest this. Then he asked, "You mean . . . they've given us no cohorts? For our sacred journey?"

"Confound the man! *Exactly!* It is a *sa*cred journey, isn't it? 'A sacred journey of Latin peace,' forget who said that, poet chap. What? *No*, no cohorts. What d'you think we need cohorts for? We've got our guards, haven't we? Purely *pro forma*, of course, but we've got 'em. Also. We've got *me*." And he drew himself up a trifle. Sir R. Tiburnus may have been a bit long in the tooth, but he was still (so his friends took good care to tell him) a fine figure of a man.

Sir Z. Sulla (whose friends did not tell him the same, and in fact, they never mentioned the matter . . . to his face, though aside, they referred to him as "Roly-poly little chap, nicest fella you'd want to meet") . . . Sir Zosimus did not seem to take utter content from this thought.

"*Me*," his companion and Brother-Superior repeated. "Who has, or need I remind you, been three times in command of Legions? Twice against the Borborygmians. And once against the Paphlagonians. So . . .''

"Yes, yes. Of course." His Junior Brother Collegiate seemed a merest bit abstracted. "Still. Hm. Should we, ah, should we take along some *beads*, perhaps? In case we have to trade with the natives?"

Sir R. Tiburnus's reply to this suggestion, tentative though it was, was both familiar and brief. He said, "*Absit omen.*"

Gaspar the Dreamer lay a-dreaming, behind his gates of horn and ivory. Then he said, without preamble, "The onyx egg." His servitors bowed silently. They brought him the onyx egg. Immense it was, and polished to a gloss, and they set it down with extreme care in its stand alongside Gaspar's bed. He gazed into it, long and long. He said, "Things do not go well."

"No, lord. Not *well*."

"Things do not go well at all."

"No, lord. No. Not at *all*."

"The Old Games are to be revived, I see."

"Yes, lord. *See*."

Curtains of dull crimson and bright black hung about the walls of the secret chamber of Gaspar the Dreamer. A whisper of incense burned.

"I like that not."

"No, lord. *Not*."

Gaspar looked once more into the onyx egg. It seemed that certain things were at move therein, but the moves, and, indeed, the form and shape of those which moved, were not clear. —Except, (perhaps) of course, to Gaspar the Dreamer. After some while he spoke again. "How can I be left full free to rule the dreams of all this Isle (though, in truth, it is no Isle at all), if the Old Ones are given offering again? They like me not. They did never."

"No, lord, no. *Never*."

Sometimes the secret chamber of Gaspar the Dreamer was round as a circle or a globe, sometimes it seemed to stand four-square, at other times it appeared triangular; and then it, as it were, was in a state of flux and nextly it had no shape for which the geometries of the AEgyptian had a name . . . and, certainly: no *Q.E.D.* Gaspar however did not care for *Q.E.D.* And neither did he care for *SPQR*. He was in no way fond of *CHI RHO*. And he shuddered at *YOD HAY VAV HAY*. All these might seem clean different things to some. To many. To most. But they had that in common in the dreams of Gaspar the Dreamer which beliked him not.

"Much of this is not strange," he said.

"No, lord. Not *strange*."

His servitors seemed of few words.

But they were of many powers.

None benign.

So.

"Yet. Something is herein odd."

"Yes, lord. *Odd*."

A silence fell. The silences of Gaspar were not like the silences of others. His silences were full of sounds. And his sounds, full of silences. He said: "Not some thing. Some one."

"Yes, lord. *One*."

"He seemed new."

"Yes, lord, *New*."

Again, the silence. Again, the sound. Gaspar

gazed into the onyx egg. He said: "Bring me the sand."

"Yes, lord. *Sand*."

The sand was brought to him in That Which We Name Not, and he blew upon it. It scattered, it darted hither and fro. It settled. A pattern lay upon the covering of the floor. "There and there. And there. Those of sullen dreams, send."

"Yes, lord. *Send*."

"And give instructions: Such and such. And such."

The sand seemed to quiver in the darkness visible.

"Yes, lord. *Such*."

Once more there was a space which was a time. And a time which was a space. And then Gaspar said: "Bring me the boards of beechwood, with the baleful signs."

To this command it was not permitted to respond by one sound. In silence they were brought, and in silence laid before him. He for a while turned his face away from the onyx egg. He gazed for a while upon the beechen boards. And then he said, "Add thereunto one name."

Somewhere a man lay dozing in a corner, neath a filthy cloak. Of a sudden he rose. And set off away from where he had been. Somewhere else a man sat bolt upright and seized his whetstone and his sword. Somewhere three men slouching in a cave not even half-awake round about a dying fire got to their knees. Felt for their knives. Went on all fours to the hole of the cave and rose upon their feet. Their hands assured them of their short and ugly little spears.

And *here* something happened, much the same. And *here*. And *there*. And *there* and *there*.

But as these men moved along all the paths along which they moved, and as they slouched or strode upon the roads they travelled, no one knew by looking at them what thoughts they had, if thoughts they had, indeed.

Only that they let their cloaks fall full around them.

As they journeyed, some, north. And, some, south. And some, others, east and west. Under the ice-bright stars. Under the chill, thin moon. Slowly and from many places far from near, could one have gazed down and seen, calculated, drawn upon a map . . . even such a map as one draws upon the sand, that they all seemed heading for one sole spot the same.

The inhabitants of New Iguvium, and, indeed, the rest of Nova Umbria—neither city nor state was very large—descended from a stock which had in its sole recorded migration exhausted all taste for innovation. There they were, there they stayed, there they intended to stay. To be sure, they no longer spoke their ancestral tongue, Latin and Greek had gradually replaced that, although they had replaced that slowly. For some years they had not worshipped their ancestral gods, that is, not openly: this had been for a while forbidden. The Nova Umbrians were of a rather placid nature: orders were orders: but when they considered either political or religious change, they were inclined, first, to be puzzled, and then to shrug their heavy shoulders. Amongst the things which caused them to puzzle and to shrug were the tidings (rather late in arriving, insofar as they might be said to have arrived at all) that there were now three Emperors in one Empire and three Persons in one God. Explanation failing these innovatory conceptions, the folk of Nova Umbria returned once again to the contemplation of the eternal verities, *viz.*, that spelt was spelt, parsnips were parsnips, parsley was parsley, and that a nice lot of chines of roasted pork after a nice session of ceremony and sacrifice was something that they rather missed.

"Ye aunciest goddes of Iguvium-in-Umbria be nocht butte dæmons," they were assured by the priests of the new religion, or religions—foreigners to a man, and speaking very odd kinds of Latin and of Greek indeed. "Ye sal in noe wisse be savèd, save ye receive Christen Baptism and commè of Lord's Day to hearè Divine Liturgie, eek y-clept ye Massè, at ye True Kirkè: *Maranatha*," concluded these missioners, ending with a word the Umbrians did not recognize at all as Latin *or* Greek and were all but certain sure was not Umbrian, either. And, when asked which church *that* was, these funny foreigners proceeded to give funny answers, as it might be, "The Marcionite," or "The Orthodox", or "The Uniate Alexandrian Gnostic." And so on.

To which the Nova Umbrians gave, generally, some such answer as, "Oh," or, "Ahah," and, also, perhaps, "Um." They allowed these new priests to come and sprinkle water on themselves and their houses (which these new priests first inspected to be sure they contained no "idols," as they called the good old harmless little images) and on their fields: no harm in a little water-magic, was there? No. And, afterwards, they gave them money. And were these new priests satisfied with this? No they were *not!*—for they had a habit of scanning the money and, often as not, casting the money away and spitting on it, offering as sole excuse that the said money

"bore upon it the imprint of an Abomination!",
when any fool could plainly see it bore upon it
nothing but an Emperor arrayed as an official god,
or something of the sort.

After a few seasons of this the Umbrians left the
new priests alone, for these new priests were clearly
crazy and the crazy were, although of course sacred
(having been touched by a god), best *left* alone; and
the Umbrians shrugged again, took the images of the
household gods out of the chests where they had been
for a while respectfully concealed; and the Umbrians
went back to copulating in the furrows to insure good
crops, as any sensible peasants would do. Except that
nowadays they did it at night, in order to avoid fuss.

The formerly annual sacred ceremonies came
and went officially unobserved, but the people of this
largely forgotten little land did on such seasons mutter to each other, "Us do miss they good gurt chunks
of good roast pork," and sigh and shrug and give a
covert and wistful glance at the formerly sacred
precincts, wherein the Christians as a matter of principle made a practice of tossing their rubbish;
naturally the people of the land and state of Nova
Umbria and City of New Iguvium were absolutely
delighted to hear that the latest new Emperor had not
only said that the sacred ceremonies might and
should be revived again but was sending them one of
the good old colleges of priests to conduct the said
ceremonies.

They turned to with right good will and cleared
up the sacred precincts from the Obelisk to the
Augurial Seats, although it was perhaps rather
naughty of them to dump the rubbish in front of the
churches, with guffaws of, "This do be thine and tha
mayst ha' it back again!" And it was there in the

sacred precincts, their camp-chairs set up nice and close to the bronze tablets with the ancient rituals incised upon them in ancient Umbrian (there was not really, as we have said, any *mod*ern Umbrian), that Sir Rufus Tiburnus and Sir Zosimus Sulla sat, crowned with garlands of flowers and plied with wine, after a triumphal welcome and following a fairly uneventful (after all) journey. The good wine had, alas, given out earlier than had been expected—it had in fact not been expected to give out at all, and the two knights had muttered about peculation and ordered their secretaries to make notes of the matter on their wax-inlaid tablets—and, rather than drink whatever swill and vinegar was by chance available along the road, they had stayed abstemious.

Fortunately this was not any longer requisite, for, after the enthusiastic chief citizens had supplied them with liquor from the mossy amphorae of best local vintages, the Quæstor himself had come forward and presented the Falernian wine intended for the ceremony; he had hidden it in his cellar, along with the bronze tablets, and the two Aetidian Brothers felt obliged to ensure themselves that it had "not gone bad in all that time," as Sir Zosimus put it.

"Doesn't seem to have," said Sir Rufus, sipping. He gazed about the scene with seemly and dignified approval. "Hope the tablets are set up in the proper old order," he said. His garland had slipped a trifle, but no one had dared mention this . . . certainly not his "Younger Brother," who was, in fact, just as slightly tipsy as he himself was. "Hope so indeed; *awesome* inscriptions on them . . . forget just what . . . ," he added.

"Not forgetting," said Sir Zosimus, feeling

rather reflective about old times, old tongues, old scenes, "nor forgetting the awesome inscription in Old Latin, on the Lapis Niger in Old Rome, '*If two black oxen make poopy here: bad luck, SPQR*' . . . of course, I translate very freely."

Sir Rufus gazed at him. Sipped. Still gazed. Said: " '*Very freely*,' you call it?"

Sir Zosimus seemed to sense a touch of something in his compeer's voice. "Yes, '*very freely*,' I call it . . . What should *you* call it?"

" '*Licentiously paraphrastic*,' is what *I* should call it."

"Oh, you should, should you?"

"Yes, I should. I *think*. 'Course, my Old Latin's a trifle rusty. May we have it again? What? Ur, *well*, I meant, have that translation again: but, no, of course not, don't mind if we have some of the Old Falernian again . . . *Mmm* . . . —Well? May we have that awesome bit about the Lapis Niger again, too?"

Sir Zosimus knit his brow, then said, " '*If two black oxen do doodoo here*—' "

Sir Rufus guffawed. " '*Doodoo*'? Moment ago it was '*poopoo*'!"

" '*Poopy*,' to be precise—"

"Fat lot you care about being precise . . . and as for your, ha ha, well, I remember at *school*, what was that boy's name?—*rus*tic boy—used to construe with more precision than *you*—and as for your, ha ha, excuse my inability to conceal my laughter, your ha ha '*bad luck, SPQR*,' well, just excuse me. Ha ha."

"*Oh?* And just *how*, might one ask, would *you*—"

"One might indeed." Sir Rufus cleared his throat; now it was his turn to knit his brow. "*I* would phrase it, ah, '*Woe upon ye, O Conscript Fathers and Assembled Plebs!*' "

Sir Zosimus made no attempt to dissemble. "Oh come. Oh come now. Oh that's rich. '*Woe upon you—*' "

" '*Ye*'!"

" '*Ye*,' then, confound it all! Admit it, now, admit it, and none of your la-de-da '*Woe upon you, ye, or yez,*' the precise words are, '*tough sow titty,*' aren't they? Well, *are*n't they?"

"Literally?"

"Well, of *course*, literally—"

"I thought you said it was 'licentiously paraphrastic.' *Ha!*"

"*What?*—'*If two licentiously paraphrastic oxen eliminate here—*'?"

"Ha ha, 'eliminate,' that's a good one. That's rich. If '*poopoo*' and '*doodoo*' were good enough for Rumulus, Romus, and Mucus Scaevola—"

" '*Muci̇us,*' *if* you don't mind."

"A detail. I *do* mind. Pædant."

"Pædant yourself. '*Mucus,*' sounds as though he couldn't wipe his *nose*—"

Sir Zosimus felt inclined to score on this one. "*Well*, matter of fact, as chap only *had* one hand and was holding a sword in it, probably *couldn't* wipe his nose: so there."

"I see no 'so there' to it: could've wiped his nose with the *back* of his one hand, sword or no s—"

"Well, if two oxen had just made ox-plop round about the Lapis Niger, probably poor old chap was more likely to want to *hold* his nose than to *wipe* it."

The two old men went into gales of laughter at this. The citizenry approved: this was more like it:

laughing and winebibbing: *Old*-time religion. The citizenry (which, nowadays, here as elsewhere, included the peasantry) had reverently left their two new and *pro tem.* priests alone, and busied themselves with such semi-sacred duties as assembling the sacrificial swine and getting ready a good bed of red-hot coals in the fire-pits, also drawing water from the old sacred well for scalding the bristles off the hogs whenever it should be time.

"Aulus Gellius says—"

"Oh, *damn* Aulus Gellius!"

"Well yes, I quite agree with you there: damn Aulus Gellius. With knobs on."

"Silly old pædant, A.G."

"Silly old pædant with knobs on."

This judgement made, a silence for a moment fell. Sir Zosimus then asked, "I say is there some more of that Old Falernian left, of course?"

"Not the way you've been slopping and sloshing it about, there isn't; no."

Sir Zosimus went a shade ruddier. "I was merely assuring meself of its acceptability before pouring the libations. And so, I observed, were *you*. None left, eh?"

The Brother-Superior leaned over, shook the amphorae—"A*fraid-not*, *pit*-ty"—shook his head, examined the label on a different amphora. "Some of the true, the blushful Hippocrene, though, you know."

"Oh? Well, nothing wrong with the true, the blushful Hippocrene, is there? Sacramentally speaking, I mean."

Sir Rufus shook his hoary head. "Not a thing wrong with it. The gods won't mind a-tall."

"Glad to get it, the gods are, me dear chap, I'll

wager, things being the way they are, Empire going to the demnition bow-wows . . . Chin-chin.''

"Lupercalia."

"Saturnalia."

"Well. Not so dusty . . . Mrumph. Shall we be getting on with it all? This north wind plays the very devil with me gout.''

"Galen says, you know, chap was telling me just the other day, Galen says playing the flute is good for the gout.''

"What, does one play the flute with one's *toes*? 'Damn Galen,' I say . . .''

"*I* say it, too. Damn Galen, with knobs on.''

The Quæstor, who had been standing by and listening, if only in a general sort of way (*This* was the way priests should talk!), now took a step forward. "If it please Your Holinesses and if Your Holinesses are quite ready, we have here on the silvern tray the offerings of fat and grain and wine, with mead optional, for the sacred offerings. And the three pregnant sows—''

Sir Rufus fixed him with a certain Look which had once quelled mutinous legions. "Well, and suppose Our Holinesses are *not* ready, what would you propose to do about it?''

The Quæstor (filled with admiration at being bullied in the high old style), clearly not being prepared to propose doing anything about it, there was a very pointed silence, interrupted by Sir Zosimus's saying, "What? '*Three pregnant sows*' on one silvern tray? Man must be *mad*, Milo of Crotona couldn't lift it—''

But his colleague's mind had fixed upon another aspect of what the Quæstor had said. " '*Mead optional*,' eh? Let's have a—''

"—Man must be mad—Eh? *'Mead optional'*? Let me see. Have a dekko at this bronze tablet with the rules incised on 'em in good old Umbrian . . . Hm. Well, by the nine gods! *'Vinu heri puni,'* sure enough: '. . . *wine, with mead optional* . . .' Well, what ought we do?"

"Have the mead brought out, is what we ought do, of course."

"Yes yes, I shouldn't wonder . . . no more of the true, the blushful Hippocrene, eh?"

The amphora was tipped, but in vain. "Not a drop of it."

"Well. *There*! Just goes to show you, wise old ways of our forefathers, valid today as the day they were inscribed on these brazen slabs: '. . . *heri puni*,' 'mead optional,' bring out the mead then, you, Quæstor, and not so damned slow about it, either. Chap is damned slow, i'n't he?"

"Damned slow, with knobs on. Wouldn't be so damned slow if he had to trot across those pits of glowing coals to get the mead, *would* he?"

"Ha ha ha!"

"Ho ho ho!"

"Quæ*stor*!"

But the Quæstor had already gone to get the mead.

SCENE: The manse of Father Fufluns, an heresiarch priest, in an hamlet. *Enter Basnobio*, assistant to same:

"You're wanted, Father Fufluns."

"Wanted for what?"

"To administer the Sacrament of Levitation, deemed illicit by the last Great Council for savoring of excessive sainthoods, as well of connection with the dead and reprobate laws of Levitical Purity, even if only homonymously. So get up.''

Basnobio had a rather curt and cynical way about him, but, so learned and generally efficient was he that, really, his superior did not know how to get along without him; Basnobio had already followed him through several sundry heresies and schisms with a loyalty which must be deemed admirable; only maybe *not*: Basnobio took *tips*!

Father Fufluns wanted his lunch, as well as other things not wanted, probably, by whomever waited now without, and was inclined to grumble. And grumble he now did. "Oh for the sake of sweet Heaven and Saint Ephraim the Deacon of Edessa (as correctly interpreted)! Never a moment's peace in this parish; how am I supposed to have time to unclothe the naked and visit the sick and cast out dæmons if people keep coming and wanting to be levitated?'' He nevertheless arose and reached for the robes his assistant was holding out.

Basnobio ("Ah, that-a Basnobio," the locals would often say, "he might-a be a bishop, sure, he have-a such-a head!" —"Yes-a, but-a Basnobio, he say-a, let-a well enough alone-a!'') Basnobio was not having any of these complaints just then. "Your Reverence should have thought of that before joining the Neognostic Heterodox Heretical Church. Your Reverence had a very promising career ahead of him in the Mixolydian Musicological Church.''

"Yes, but the Mixolydian hierarchy were so toffy-nosed, called me a whoremonger and a pæderast and a simonizer and I can't remember what else they didn't call me . . . *and they said I sang off-key!* Now, that, as you well know, Basnobio, *that* is a *lie*! I merely did not invariably sing in the Mixolydian

Mode, is all. Matter of *con*science; ah well, man
wants but little here below, nor wants that little long,
is what I always say, and if a man cannot sing as the
Spirit moves him, well—'' His voice was by now
slightly muffled by reason of having to penetrate
several layers of robes, including the so-called Mantle
of Elijah: a vestment not indeed absolutely required
by the canons and rubrics of the Neognostic
Heterodox Heretical Church, he had picked it up
whilst briefly dallying with the doctrines of the
Church of the Former and the Latter Rains (Ebionite
Division), but had not felt moved by the Spirit to
accept the Sacrament of Circumcision. The so-called
Mantle of Elijah consisted of exceptionally thick
sheepskin, very utile in the wintery regions of, say,
Upper Sarmatia, but merely picturesque and damnably itchy in the more summery climates to the south.
still: Levitation . . . Elijah had gone *up* . . . hadn't
he?

    ''Ready now,'' said Father Fufluns.

    Peregrine had followed as the branches of the
trees had indicated he should, and the following had
at first been slightly difficult, for there lay upthrust
at this first point between the trees an abrupt shelving
of sheer rock. It was, fortunately, not particularly
high and not particularly rough, and, fortunately,
the hooves of his horse marked it but little (perhaps,
save to some eye as keen as that of the legendary
Athenian, not at all: and the legendary Athenian,
were he still around at all, was certainly not around
here, was probably far away in deep discussion with
the Talmudic Sages of Sura and Pumbaditha,
discussing the recondites of the egg laid on the Sab-
bath, and the malignant habit of certain sectaries of

lighting false beacon fires in pretension of having seen the New Moon). This outcropping of the barebones of the earth gave way after a while to the forest true, and, obedient always to the waving branches, Peregrine followed through the forest.

The forests . . .

Forests of oak, forests of pine, oak for goodly furnitures and the keels and timbers and the great ribs of ships, oak for wine barrels. Pine for tar and planks for said ships and pitch to caulk them with. Pine for resin to pour into the oak barrels to keep the air from the wine and so to keep the wine from souring. Pine for kindling for a quick flame; oak for the great glowing beads of coal like lumps of amber, beds of glowing coals to last the night and roast the ox. A many generation of pine planks would come and go in any one boat and ship, but the oak timbers were forever. Well, almost forever: when the oak went, the vessels went, too. For quickness and haste and rapid service: pine. For endurance, oak.

Presently Peregrine saw, for one, that the branches were wavering rather than waving. And, for another, that he was on some slight semblance of a road, high and heavy grew the grass thereon, but, clear: a road.

Where the road might lead, and he hoped it might lead him to his friends the folk of Alfland, for, though he had not known them for long, they were all the folk he did in this distant land know; *whither* the road might take him was of importance, but more important was which way was he to take the road?

There was no wind he felt, but, as though there were a wind the smaller trees inclined their trunks, and the larger trees moved their branches no thicker than the slender trees. Moved them, slowly, and he supposed, for one last time. Moved them towards the right. Peregrine gave them all one last and loving salute, heard one loving and last rustle, hum and thrum. He turned his horse's head to the right.

He had scarce gone a league, or maybe not even half-a-league, when he heard a voice call. "*Halt.* Pass on at your *per*il," said the voice. It was a reedy, wavery voice, and if it did not indeed lack all conviction, well, certainly it lacked much. Peregrine looked ahead, he looked right, he looked left, and realizing that he had been looking at his own eye-level, he next looked *up*: nothing.

So he looked *down*.

And there, reclining more than somewhat rather wearily under a bush of sweet lavender, he observed the oldest, be-draggledest, most woebegone-looking sphynx that he had ever encountered; smeared with cheap eye-paint which had more than just begun to run, and smelling of very stale patchouli.

"*Well!*" said Peregrine. Ought his flesh to have crawled? There was after all no visible cliff over which the sphynx might have thrown him, as was (supposedly) the very bad habit of sphynxes (Appledore had once insisted that the proper plural was *sphynges*, but Appledore was not here—and of a sudden Peregrine missed the learned and utterly idiosyncratic old man very much: in vain). "Well, well, *well*. —Aren't you supposed to ask me a question?" he asked.

"Well, *hon*estly," said the sphynx. "I mean, *ac*tually. Of *course* I'm supposed to ask you a question!" Its manner was very slightly petulant, but some other emotion overlay the petulance. "The truth is, if you *really* want to *know*," the sphynx said, moodily, "is that I've run *out* of questions to

ask." And its lower lip quivered, and a tear ran out
of each eye, further smearing its eye-paint, which
really was in no state to stand much more smearing.
And it sniffled. And then it said, "You don't happen
to know any good *rid*dles, I suppose?" This was,
after all, it really *was* a question. But it was asked
without much hope.

"I used to have a very *good* question, I mean,
*rid*dle, and it used to fool oh just *oodles* of people.
And then that damned *Greek*—"

"Theseus?"

"Was that his name? Oh, I don't care what his
name was, really, but he went on and just told, well,
simply, *ev*erybody, what the answer *was*. And things
have never been the same since. People used to *laugh*
when they'd see me, after that. Even before I'd had a
chance to ask." And it put its head under its wing
and blew its nose. Then the head emerged again, and
regarded Peregrine with brighter eyes. "*Hmmm?*" it
asked.

"Well, I don't know if I ought to," Peregrine
said, thoughtfully, fingering his fairly new-grown
moustache (it really was a moustache by now, and
not a mere line of dark down). "Besides, I'd thought
he'd killed you—"

The sphynx clicked its tongue. "Oh, I was just
*sham*ming. I just *play*ed dead. Imagine! He actually
tried to kill me! The *rat!*"

"Well? Hadn't you tried to kill him? And other
people? If they couldn't answer your silly old
riddle?"

It was with something like astonishment that the
sphynx now looked up. " '*Kill* people'? Oh for pity's
sake: *no!* Of course they'd had to pay a *pen*alty: but
that wasn't the penalty! And I don't know what

made that Greek so hoity-toity . . . I *mean*, AFTER
ALL!''

"Oh, well," said Peregrine. He thought a
moment. "A riddle, hey?" The sphynx regarded him
with bird-bright eyes. "Hey!" exclaimed Peregrine.
"How about this one? 'What is it that has four legs
and flies?' ''

The sphynx huddled itself together, frowned
fiercely, concentrated. A while passed. Then the
sphynx said, " *'What is it that has four legs and
flies?'* You can't, I suppose, mean another sphynx?
No, that would be too easy. A, a griffin? *No?* Oh.
Oh *my*! A pegasus?''

Peregrine said that that was closer, but it wasn't
quite right.

"Well," the sphynx said, more briskly than
usual; "I give *up*. I surrender. Besides, none of those
answers seemed very good at *all*. Very well. What
does have four legs and flies?''

"A dead horse.''

The sphynx blinked. Then it licked one toe and
moistened one eyebrow with it. Then it placed one
wing-feather alongside its nose. Then it winked.
Then it suddenly began running around in circles,
flapping its wings and cackling with delighted glee.
Then it flew up into the air and circled round and
round and round about; then, and in a most abrupt
manner, flew down again. "Something the matter,"
asked Peregrine, concerned for the creature.

But he need not have been.

"*Pssst*," the sphynx said. "Are you by any
chance being followed by a band of armed men,
bearing a banner with the blazon of a clenched fist?''

"*Zeus*-piter," said Peregrine. "Well, I don't
know for sure. I mean, I might *be*. I hadn't planned

to be. I wonder if that was what the dryads had been warning me about? Uh . . . are they *close*?''

"*Welll* . . .'' The sphinx looked at him a moment with a look in its eye. Then the sphinx sighed. ''Oh, not really. I *was* going to tell you a big fib, and then I was—but I won't. So there. No. Not what you'd call *close*. But. I am afraid. Enjoy your company though I do, and I *do*. The longer we spend in these moments of delightful conversation, well, the closer they may *get*. And, whilst this may mean *one* thing for *me*, it may, I am afraid, mean quite another thing for *you*. So,'' and here another tear trickled down the sphinx's cheek, ''*off* you *go*. —You'll never *know* what you've done for me!''. And, as Peregrine, with a wave of his hand, started to move along, the sphinx, with a flap of its wings, came flying up and gave him a quick, a very quick embrace, and a quick, a very quick, kiss. And then flew not merely down, but away; and out of sight.

Peregrine raised his hand to touch the place. It was, alas, both wet and smeary. But he was grateful enough, and man enough, not to wipe it away till he was well out of sight.

Once again he attempted to make his mount move faster.

And, once again, in fact, as always, his mount moved no faster than its slow, accustomed pace.

And, meanwhile, inasmuch as the free observation and celebration of any religion, including, once again, that of Pagan religion, had been made free and void of persecution and penalty by Himself the August Caesar Dux Imperator et sic cætera: what of Sapodilla, where still lived and reigned King Paladrine, father of Peregrine? Inasmuch as

Sapodilla had always been and always remained largely forgotten and entirely Pagan: of Sapodilla, therefore: Nothing.

The dragon Smarasderagd was leisurely gliding along at a very high, and consequently, very safe altitude, when he became somewhat suddenly aware of something which much misliked him; that is, not to be needlessly archaic or obscure, he became aware of something which the dragon Smarasderagd much misliked: to say (as, indeed, we *have* said) that it "much misliked him" is to be indeed guilty of what some have called, and indeed still call *the pathetic fallacy*: id est, to personify Nature and to attribute thereunto qualities purely human: oh, well. And this something he described to himself, in a ritually in-cantatory mutter, as "Strong head winds from north northwest, expected soon to reach gale force . . ."—"Soon," at any rate, at that particular altitude.

Now, it is not that the dragon absolutely could not fly into the headwinds, but, after all, for how long could even a dragon keep that up? The effort (he considered, reflectively and calculatedly) . . . the energy . . . He had already disposed of the Treasure Bags of Alfland, *where*, it was for him to know and humans to find out, and now he had other things on his mind. He thought of these things, even as he thought of these new other things; and the thoughts of a long and scaly dragon are long and scaly thoughts, and he felt immediately obliged to consider his options—some have traced this last phrase to Cataline's Oration Against Cicero, others scoff at this and point to a certain clause in the Addendum to Pliny the Third: but, in the long run: who *cares*?

Should he go, the while these high winds lasted, the sort which sweep the sky of clouds e'en though the children of men as they wearily till the earth for bread (or perish) scarcely notice, for rest and shelter to and in a craggy cave he knew of? *no!* "Filthy stinking hole, some dragons have *no* sense of the elements of sanitation, and it's a dirty dragon which fouls its own lair . . . or anyone else's lair for that matter . . . or even a lair which, belonging to no one in particular, is after all *every*one's lair . . ."

Something now seemed nibbling at the edges of the dragonic mind, and he considered upon the thought as he essayed trial flights at different levels in order to see if avoiding the headwinds (let alone the gales) were possible . . . and then the thought came into full center: somewhere on or close abaft the pineal eye: "*Ballast!*" he cried. "I must take on ballast!"—chuckling and shaking his scaly ("squam-ous," if you prefer; *we* do *not*) head in self-reproach at having for so long overlooked the obvious.

Ballast. A large rock might just do. One large enough, but not, of course, *too* large. A log. Or, as it may be, a sheep. Or an ox. He might carry any of these in his claws. It would all depend.

And he began to look down and round and all about very, very keenly.

"*Mead*. Took your own bloody time about it, I must say. *Hmmm* . . . Not bad mead. Eh?" said the Rev. Sir Zosimus Sulla.

"Not bad mead at all," the Rev. Sir Rufus Tiburnus concurred. "*Well*. Suppose we must get on with it; be here all day and all night, else. Let me see, now." He squinted at the bronze tablets containing the directions for the sacred rituals, quoted,

" 'Sacrifice to Jupiter Grabovius . . .' "

" 'Jupiter *Grabovius*'?"

"Says *here*; have a dekko yourself, if you don't believe me: 'Sacrifice to Jupiter Grabovius . . . Sacrifice to Trebus Jovius, and, ah, ah, what's all this? *Ah!* —Sacrifice to *Mars* Grabovius (local deities assimilated to the State Cultus, must be respectful no matter how odd they sound, else the natives might get restless and we shan't be able to stay the night; can't have the natives getting restless) . . . And . . . and . . . I say, what's it say down here, no, confound it, *here*: all these squiggly little letters . . .'"

Sir Zosimus peered closely. "Says, '*Pray in a murmur, sacrifice with mead.*' "

"No more mead. 'Three pregnant sows,' yes. Hear them squealing? But—mead? No more mead. See for yourself. No more mead."

"Well, *get* some more mead, then, I say! Quæstor!"

The Quæstor approached but a bit more closely. "Pray pardon, Your Holinesses," he said, very diffidently, "but the correct reading of that last line is '*meal*' . . . not '*mead*' . . ."

"Precious lot *you* know about a correct reading," said Sir Rufus, with warmth. "—Shifty looking fellow, i'n't he?"

"Shifty looking fellow with knobs on. —who *got* those sows pregnant, I should like to know? Bring out the mead, I say!"

"I say so, too—"

The Quæstor scurried off, Sir Rufus calling after him, "And give some to the local Conscript Fathers, silly old dotards if ever I saw some, it will help wash the mustard out of their moustaches—"

"Yes, quite. I say, you Quæstor, fetch out all

the mead there is—and give some to the local Plebs, too. —Eh?'' He turned and faced his Sacred Brother.

Who at once said, ''By all means give some to the Plebs, too. Give lots of some to the Plebs. Backbone of the State, the Plebs, what?''

Sir Zosimus nodded so vigorously that his garland slipped e'en more askew. ''Backbone of the State, with knobs on . . . What's it say next?''

The Very Reverend Sir Rufus Tiburnus concentrated on the exceedingly awesome syllables of the exceedingly obsolete Umbrian language (Hieratical Version). ''Says, *'Sevaknis persnihmu pert spinia isunt klaves persnihmu.'* Well, *that* seems simple enough: *'Spit ceremonially, pray on the other side of the Obelisk (or Simulacrum) on the spinial, and,'* hmm, hmm . . . *What*? *'At the same spot he shall pray with the* smearing-sticks . . .'?''

''I fail to share your simplistic view. *I* read it—*obviously*—*'With the ceremonial spits he shall pray on the other side of the Obelisk, etc.'* ''

His sacred and reverend colleague peered again. ''Eh? Oh. Hm. Well. Praps you're right . . . Well, and how do you construe, *isunt klavles persnimhu*, haw haw. *'At the same spot he shall pray with the smearing-sticks.'* Silly of me, what? How do you construe?''

''I construe, *'At the same spot he shall pray with the smearing-sticks.'* ''

Sir R. Tiburnus stared at him, aghast. '' *'—with* the *smear*ing-sticks'?''

''Or in other words, *'Anoint the Obelisk'* (or, if you prefer, *'the Simulacrum'*) . . .''

''If I were to tell you what I should *real*ly prefer, th' immortal gods might strike me dead.''

''Serve you jolly well right, too, probably . . .

Well, well, let us see what's the rest of this part. *Veskles snate asnates*, oh dear *me*! '*Vessels snotty and unsnotty*.' Well, speak about 'rude forefathers,' this beats anything!''

Sir the Very Reverend Rufus Tiburnus said, more than a trifle smugly, " '*Vessels wet and unwet*,' mean to say, '*—and dry*,' is surely the correct reading here in any but a slavishly literal sense—"

"Oh get *on* with it, for pity's sake, there are no wreaths for rhetoric being handed out here."

His colleague shrugged, continued his readings from the bronze tablets. " '*With the ceremonial vessels wet and dry he shall pray at the Obelisk*' (or *Simulacrum*, if you prefer, or even if you don't). '*He shall pour a libation and dance the* tripudium. *He shall anoint the Simulacrum*' (or *Obelisk*), *and*— '*where are those confounded wooden spoons*? —'*smearing-sticks*' indeed!—'*and pray with the ceremonial unguent, and wash his hands away from the altar. He shall return from the altar,*'—no, confound it,—'*to the altar; at the altar he shall pray silently with ceremonial wine.*' There is no ceremonial wine left—"

"*Pray* for some, then."

"I fail to share your exceedingly questionable piety . . . '*Struglas fiklas sufafias kumaltu kapire punes vepuratu*,' oh gods! Is there no *end* to this? Say what one will 'bout the Christians, common cultists and silly sectarians though they be, still, they pray in Latin or Greek,—oh *bad* Latin, I grant you, and worse Greek: *but still and all*! Ah well: *Um*brian. One has one's duty, one *does* it: backbone of the Imperium: Immortal Rome, Live Forever . . . Blibble blibble blabble blabble, tum-te-tum, fiddle-de-*de*, '*And the dog*,' *dread*ful thing, sacrificing a *dog*; for-

tunately commuted ages ago, so . . . which is to
say—'*the hog*,' which is to *say*, one trotter of *one*
hog, '*shall be buried at the altar. Lucius Tetteius, son
of Titus, approved the foregoing in his
quæstorship.*' ''

"Wretched fellow . . . Still . . . changed *dog* to
hog, chap can't be *all* bad.''

"Never said he *could*; backbone of the State,
these native Quæstors. What's the next bit there?''

'' '*And the Aetidian Brothers,*' that's you and
me, you know, '*are required to give to the Clavernii
at the Festival ten portions of pickled pork and five
portions of roasted goat-meat, and the Clavernii,*'
whoever *they* are—''

"Backbone of the State.''

'' '—*are required to give to the Aetidian
Brothers six pounds of choice spelt, cumquat taxea
lardum, or some such piffle . . .*' *Well*. They'll take
roasted pork, like it, lard it, or lump it; if they want
goat, let them go chase one; and they can bloody well
keep their choice spelt to make up the difference.
'*Choice spelt*,' what should we do with spelt
nowadays, might I ask?''

"I feed it to me peacocks, back home, what *I* do
with it.''

"Oh, do you have peacocks, back home?

"Yes I do. Dreadful noisy birds they are, and I'd
poison them all, 'cept that they annoy me wife, only
reason I've *got* 'em.''

"Well, well: and, fancy, I never knew. Well,
would *you* like the spelt?''

"No no no. Thousand thanks. Very kind of you.
Can buy it cheaper in the market, back home.''

''. . . well, *that's* settled, then . . . *Or*, hmm, suppose we *could* translate this bit as '*beech-cured ham*'

or '*fat bacon*,' although, must admit, the Umbrian *h* is a difficulty—''

"The Umbrian *h* is a *damned* difficulty, trouble with the Umbrian *h*, you want to know. —*Out of the question!* Roast pork, good enough for anyone; good enough for Homer: good enough for *me*, *you*, and certainly for these chaps. '*Pickled pork,*' indeed, la-de-da: just watch 'em gobble up the good old roasted when the time comes!''

From place to place behind the semi-ruinous spinal-wall a number of small boys had all this while been concealed, running message relays; one of them now came sloping up to where the Conscript Fathers, who had seldom had all the mead they could drink, were sitting in front of the Plebs, who had *never*—or, at any rate, never before—had all the mead *they* could drink; one of the former addressed the small boy.

"Ah, my little man, and what are the august and distinguished visiting clergy declaiming at this point of the sacred ritual?''

The little man could hardly have cared less about the Umbrian *h*, the anointing-spoons, or all the rest of it; besides, he was rather far along down the relay, and little of the finer points had reached him anyway; his answer was succinct. "Roast pork, Gaffer.''

This message spread like lightning amongst all the assembled. There followed instant declarations of, "Ah, roast pork! Roast pork! *That's* the old time religion, and it's good enough for me!'' And the few of the few local Christians who had dared the ecclesiastical anathema to come close enough to listen and, now and then, peek (and to observe, with great disappointment, the total absence of lions and so, hence, their chances of martyrdom), scowled and sneered behind their hands, and bit their beards with bitterness.

The particular path on which Peregrine now found himself was so overgrown that the horse needed scarcely stop to graze; it sufficed the beast merely to slow down a trifle, if slower (Peregrine wondered) were possible, and snaffle up the grass as it poked along. Indeed the thought had come into Perry's mind that he might well go faster were he to leave his horse behind: but two things dissuaded him: for one, it would have been better to have done so sooner, where the animal might merely have wandered off into plowland and thus offer no clue: but *now*, if found, it would stand out like a elephant—and, for another, it was after all not *his*, Perry's horse, and ill could King Alf spare it. And so, with a sigh—

—his sigh, however, was interrupted by two actions, both emanating from the horse. (Perry had never learned its name; from time to time and general principles he had addressed it as Dobbin, but, for all the good this did he might as well have called it Crumback, Sookey, or Fido): first the horse paused and raised its tail, and for no such purpose as keeping the sun out of its rider's eye; then the horse proceeded to pour an immense libation; then the horse broke wind with a sound like . . . well, if not precisely like thunder, at least like the sound of the thunder-machine in one of your better equipped amphitheaters, does the script call for it . . . the horse raised its ponderous head, and first it cried Ha Ha; then it neighed; then it made a few sounds as if to say, For this relief, much thanks. And *then*, and to Perry's absolute astonishment (still, he kept hold of such items of harness and horse-gear as he might), the horse broke into something much like a ponderous trot; a gallop, no, one could not call it a gallop . . . not really . . .

Has Your Seruant to Command ("Abel Scrivener," let us call him) already indited some such line, as, it might be, "It seemed to Peregrine that he had been taking one side road and by-road after another, and for quite some time, now; he had no real idea at all where he was, but he was well off the main-travelled roads, and well he knew it . . ."? If so: get on with it. If not: take the will to equal the deed, and the line as read.

Perhaps the unaccustomed hard-riding had shaken Perry's brains, but for whatever reason, shaken up he did feel, and in a rather odd way to which he could put no name. How long had he *been* on this horse, anyway?—he had no idea. He did, however, have the idea that, pursuit or not, it would be far from amiss were he to dismount; and this he did, stretched his cramped legs and swung his arms (one by one, for he switched the bridle from hand to hand), and he yawned and blinked and kicked the cramp from either leg . . .

He became aware that he had been feeling thirsty, and he knew that his leather bottle had been a long while empty, although he shook it next his ear to make sure: it had been a long time empty. Well; and if he were thirsty, so must be the horse . . . an inference from minor to major, or was it from major to minor? Well, it depended on this: was the horse *major* by virtue of size, or was *Perry* major by reason of his possessing one more faculty of reason than the horse . . . Appledore, who had at the Court of

Sapodilla acted as Peregrine's tutor as well as astrologer, sorcerer, philosopher, augur, *a capella* bard and the gods knew what else; Appledore would have taken great delight in such an argument and exercise in rhetoric: but Appledore was not here, Appledore had stayed behind, along with not-so-daft Claud, that other native of Sapodilla who had accompanied Peregrine on the first stage of his Grand Tour, stayed behind in Chiringirium, enjoying the warm hospitality of Darlangius G., its newest Caesar . . . and Perry had not.

Ah well.

So he looked for water. This back-road had certainly borne no imperial posting-party for long and long and long; no carts of merchandise had worn the weeds out of its overgrown ruts in many and well a day. There were no more huge and vasty trees, second-growth at best the timber was, and beneath and behind the shrubble and the stubble and the thistle in the overgrown fields he could see more than one evidence of fallen-down (when not indeed burnt-down) latifundia. Horse ambling on ponderously behind him, Perry picked his way along broken bricks and grass-grown gravel and even pavings of stone. He found here a well: the well was stopped up with stones, one passing swarm of looters and wreckers had seen well that the nexting swarm would slake no thirst *there*. He sought for conduits, the conduits had fallen in, were still moist and green, but no shovel was there to delve and make depth of water with. There were certainly enough sunken cellars with and without crumbled walls to have filled with water in the wet season: but now was the wet season not. Peregrine sighed again; then a thought came to him: could he find a willow twig? but no: dowsing-

rod or not, still he would need dig and delve . . . well
. . . if the water were perhaps very near the surface,
perhaps a sharpened stick . . .

A wall by no means fallen was straight in front
of him, and, as he could not go through it, he would
needs go around it; he turned right and . . . stopped.

For a moment he could not even fathom *why* he
had stopped; nor, as he felt himself swinging left,
could he imagine *why* he was swinging left. Surely he
was more tired by far than he had thought . . . *Ah!*

He was swinging left because the horse was
swinging left: therefore . . . therefore *what*? Best
follow the horse, for at any rate one of them knew
where he was going, and where he wanted to go: and
that one was the horse. And the horse neighed again
and the horse whinnied and the horse quickened his
pace.

Ahead lay a pond. Perry thought, first of all,
that he would now be able to drink. And (he
thought), after that, he might even be able to have a
swim: if the pond were not deep enough, well, he
might at any rate kneel in it and splash. Off not too
far in the distance he saw some large outcroppings of
rocks, porous, perhaps, certainly with holes in them
visible even from here. At once he forgot them: he
and horse were at the water. The horse waded in,
snorting, and dipped his muzzle. Peregrine knelt at
the barm and cupped his hands and drank. And
drank. And—

He was still drinking even as he began to wriggle
out of his clothes. Then he gave over drinking, his
first thirst slaked, and got well and altogether out of
the green tunicle and the trews with the large brown
check; then he got well into the water, although he
shivered with pleasure as the cool and cold and wet of

it began to tickle his tiny hairs, before he could stoop even to cover his hams and splash his breast and shoulders. He intended to go further in, but simple fatigue got the better of him, he simply sat down and sat back, and once again he sighed. But it was a simple sigh.

And so, sitting, he looked around him. People were after all still living hereabouts, he had seen them not and heard them not, he saw no signs of whatever men and women they might be: but there: and there: and *there*: on the muddy parts of the banks of the pond, he saw their children's footprints.

And then he saw the children, and he began a smile and a gesture of friendship—

—and finished neither—

Child-size they were. But they were not children.

Children at two feet high, or even perhaps at most three, children have neither breasts a-pout or a-dangle, nor have children beards and body-hair.

His blood chilled, his heart swelled, the flesh prickled and his tiny hairs stood out; his every muscle tensed: could he at one dash make for his horse (he never gave a *thought* to his clothes) and mount—

Would the horse have taken flight along with him? Would he even have reached the horse? These Weefolk had arrows and had bows: they did not even nock one in the other. They had spears, of a sort, the small, small, small very small folk: they did not throw them. For one long moment all stood still. The water did not even ripple. Then he saw them pointing at him, then he saw them lay their weapons down, then he heard them make the oddest sound that ever he had heard—and saw how they made it—by cupping their hands to their armpits and pumping their arms. It was, in a way, a welcome. In a way, it was, an applause. And then they spoke.

Why, we saw upon thee the mark of safe-pass-age made by our sisterbrother the Smynx, said one, said more than one, when Peregrine came at last to ask. (By and by he realized the Weefolk could never pronounce an *f* or *ph* when it followed an *s*: And would (thought he) they had no greater problem.) Perry could no more than blink at this, they smiled a bit—they almost never laughed, nor made other loudly sounds—and touched him . . . Several, after the first bold touch, made bold enough to touch him, too: others did not . . . not then, not ever . . . He felt where their tiny fingers felt: enough trace of the Sphynx's eye-paint and scented facial unguents and ointments remained upon a cheek. *But canna thu no' guess we smellet thee first?*

"I daresay," said Perry, wryly. But the wryness was wasted. As for any sneer or jeer, or even tolerant chuckle or embarrassed explanation of what had been . . . or had not been . . . between him and the Sphynx: there was no such need, no need for such; no—in fact—even thought of such. Sphynx was Sphynx. Weefolk were Weefolk. The small smile was merely at his, Perry's, forgetfulness that the sign (or smear) was still, in remnants, on his cheek at all.

It was warm enough in the pelts they'd given him,—given him for warmth, for they themselves were naked and they knew it not . . . or, at any rate, cared about it not,—whilst his clothes lay a-soak in some crudely dammed pool in a creek, along with some saponiferous herb. He didn't even know what pelts they were, save that, hair-side inside, it was warm enough in them. Some pan of bark sat alongside him with something in it, he knew not what, it was food, from time to time he dipped and

ate. Talk was not incessant; silence was not in-
terminable; he knew that the horse was penned safe
within some rocky cleft, knew that none of his Alvish
friends had come this way . . . he had not really
thought they had, unless they'd circled, still . . . they
might have circled . . . and so for the moment he felt
safe and warm. And, slightly, drowsy.

A Weewoman was speaking now, speaking soft
and low: he listened. *Och, the Gotha push down the
Roma and the Roma push down the Kelta and the
Kelta push down the Weefolk; thu knowedd this;
thu knowedd the Weefolk be we* . . . Indeed they *were*
wee, though scarcely hop-o'-my-thumb wee; Perry
realized that if one had to live in holes in the rock, it
was a great help to *be* wee . . . *We study, och, what
arts we may, here in the greeny wood . . . We ferm
not, for why 'ould we ferm? So they 'ould take our
crops, och, ond ot lahst, our lahnd? If we did ought
in metal 'ork, 'ould they not see ond smell the forge-
smoke ond hear the clong of metal, metal-on? We
gother the small fruits o' the soil, the thucket, the
forest and the fens . . . the scronnel herbs ond the
rune-thorns, the rune-roots ond the magic mosses . . .
ond we 'ork in thot sort wise . . . we spin spells, we
weave webs, we moil in magic; these be our arts, such
are our crops, in this wise 'lone do we ferm and delve
and forge* . . .

There was a question, at least one question, no:
at least two: by logical extension: three . . . in his
mind. But a great drowse was upon him, and . . .
and . . .

Ahsk it, gigont, said a Weeman.

In the dimlight, Perry strove to form some
several thoughts. A few were simple. "Does bale or
bane lie yet behind me? Does bane or bale lie yet

before me? And can I even somewhat avoid the
same?''
    Yes. Ond—
    Yes. Ond—
    Somewhat.
He slept.

    It was day, and sans the bone-cold of dawn, but,
it being somewhat overcast, more than this, in wise
of time, he could not say. They had rigged him a
boothie or a bower of branches, roofed with rough-
thatch bound in bundles; now, he being heard or seen
(or even, perhaps and still, to smell . . . he had
washed, perhaps only in his mind did the faint, stale
odor of patchouli and the gods-know-what still cling)
to move, once again the tiny figures came out of the
mists: fewer than before; he was by now less of a
curiosity and wonder. And they brought him chest-
nut ground in a quern and mixed with honey-and-
water. And he ate.
    And then he talked. He had been so silent before
on all his long way, with none to hearken, save himself, the Trees, the Sphynx, and the horse; so now
perhaps he babbled more than—
    But they listened.
    ''I suppose, I am sure, there is no clepsydra
among you, nor am I myself accustomed to marking
much the hours; generally I let the cock and the ass
do that, the one by his crowing and other by his bray-
ing . . . and such a thing as a calendar, why it's so
long since I've seen one I can tell neither calends
from ides nor ides from gules . . . and yet, I confess,
there is somewhat and something which confuses me
about the matter of time . . . of latterly . . . of now
. . .'' And he stroked his beard. Perhaps it really was

thicker than before, but he was after all of an age
when the beard after long quiescence does grow swift
and thick in no great time . . .

Och, gigont . . . Gigont, och . . .

They seemed to speak to him in turns . . . and
even so, with some almost-difficulty . . . clearly,
from the hesitations, the pauses, the matter was not
one of customary and frequent talk . . . and yet there
was no confusion amongst them . . . in the matter . . .
thus:

*Hast thu not heard, gigont, thy philosophers tell
thot there be seven, or be they eight, and what motter
and who care . . . not we . . . some certain number of
zones which engirdle the yarth . . . that these be girds
or belts of clime . . . but it seem thot they have no'
taught, ond so we must suppose a-neither have they
larned of one other zone . . . of one, at least, other
. . . these girds, or belts, or zones, ha' it so: these
eight or seven poss round about this ball of dung on
which we live, they poss from left to right, from right
to left . . .*

*But tother belt: no. For tis the belt, no' of clime,
but of time, ond it posseth round about ye tother
way, from pole to pole ond no' from sunbright to
sundim . . . it toucheth but here and there, but lightly
. . . for tis in some measure moved by the moon, and
the moon is but lightly moving, for the moon is but
planet of way . . . but it toucheth ever in yander
countryside . . . and whosoever and whensoever
posseth by ond through, why he and she cometh as
twere from oneday to notherday . . . mayhop from
one moon to nothermoon . . .*

*. . . we should not, och, gigont, were we thee,
move the heart much about it . . . is there ought thu
const do to change it? A-nay. None. Argo, forbear to*

fret. What con be done, ond we shall do it: it be thus:

And whilst the *thus* was still in preparation,
down the narrow path between one cleft in the rocks
and another (the latter serving as way to the world
at large) came the horse: and he looked not only
fresher for his night's rest but fresher than he had
ever looked: coat glossy, hooves cleaned, even the
feather-hair-clumps above his hooves all smooth and
free of clots of mud. The beast was not sore-backed
nor saddle-galled, and his mane was well-combed,
with flowers braided into it. And, inasmuch as there
were no other horses round about, and no reason to
think that the Weefolk served regular stints in someone's stable, Peregrine bethought him thoughtfully
that an art than mere grooming may well have been
at work . . .

He thanked them on behalf of the horse; whilst
yet he was so doing, out came water-bottles of good
size and well-carved of wood with wooden stopples,
came out basket of berries fresh and berries dried,
parched grain and dried muskrooms and dried wild-
apples, these last so fragrant that Perry felt, almost,
he could live upon the smell of them alone.

He was extending his thanks when he observed
some other tasks going on, and, so soon as he had
finished his courtesies, he turned to observe what
these might be: great hampers woven of withy-withes
were being fetched along, and, amidst much mutter-
ings, being emptied on the road in the direction
whence he had come; when he made but an half-step
to go look closelier, he was stopped. Stopped pol-
itely, but: stopped. The Weefolk were, indeed, wee.

They were also . . . strong.

"Oh, I'm sorry if I—" Peregrine began. But
apologies were not expected. What were expected

were explanations, and these his hosts at once gave him.

The bane and bale which pursueth thee consist in men upon harses and in men upon foot; they be not many, only one hond and one finger: but they be armed.

It took him but a moment to realize that *six* was the number of his pursuers; as to how this or any of this was known, he asked not. He felt he ought not ask anything at all, and, indeed, the explanations continued without his questioning.

Thu see'st yander thorns. Indeed he did, saw them full well even from where he stood, no more prickles of the berry-bush or the rose—, but great thick spurs like those on wild cockerels. *These be thucket-thorns of certain kind. These be rune-thorns we be scottering on the road behind thee. They will be, och, costing spells upon the harses of the men of bale and bane, and will make them walk in circles. When the men of bale and bane dismount to see what reason, they . . . ond those already afoot . . . they shall walk in circles, too—och! They shall walk widdershins till they drop, till they die . . . or till the spell be braken: which be the same thing . . .* ''

So it was that Peregrine left the wee-people-who-live-in-the-hills, who, owing him nought, had given him much. For long and for long had they been driven further and further and deeper and deeper; for how long this their present respite might last, he could not know. The great conquests of the world occur like claps of thunder: and in this latest silence, as Empire crumbled, for a while at least the wee ones would have peace.

Presently he left both woods and hills behind him, and, descending, found the road, which showed

signs of being more travelled than before, and began
to lead him through a land as flat, almost, as an offering of unleavened bread.

But before he had quite reached the level plain
he had seen lying at no very great distance away, if
not a city, at least a town, or—if not quite a town, or
even a village, at least a hamlet.

He took a deep breath. And he rode on.

As anyone who was really anyone was watching
the Sacred Ceremony (saving of course the few local
Christians, who were under an episcopal anathema
not to attend) (and the even fewer local Jews, who
would not have attended anyway: one of these,
named Reuben, was at this very moment asking
another one, named Simeon, if there was or was not
basically a difference between Christianism and
Paganism; Simeon answered that there certainly was,
to wit, the same difference that there was if the rock
fell on the pitcher or the pitcher fell on the
rock)—since almost everyone was in the center of
New Iguvium, the capital—such as it was—of Nova
Umbria, scarcely anyone was around to observe the
gradual gathering of a certain number of men under
the arches of what had once been the Stoa. There was
a certain furtiveness in their gathering, there, a certain . . . one might say . . . secretiveness . . . which,
since they were quite alone, seemed rather superfluous. Had anyone been present to see them, anyone
would have observed that, somewhat oddly, they
were all cloaked. And someone might have observed
that as, from time to time, one of them moved, which
was not often, here and there was disclosed a bulge
. . . which might have been a sword . . . or a javelin
. . . or, even, at least, a knife . . .

As it happened, and to be quite precise, they were *not* quite alone; "anyone who was really anyone" and "scarcely anyone" does not exclude absolutely everyone: someone else *was* there, and that was the local blind man. This one, whose name, which he had himself almost forgotten, was Pappus, had usually a small boy to guide him round the town: but today the small boy, curse him! had forsaken his duty in order to be one of the relay-messengers, and so Pappus, finding himself forgotten, had gotten so far as at least one familiar spot, a sheltered niche lying opposite the Stoa, and here he had sate him down to wait. He had not much: but of patience; and of this he had aplenty.

The arrival of these newcomers, quietly though they arrived, had not by him passed unnoticed; from time to time Pappus had lifted up his cracked old voice and uttered his familiar plea and plaint of "Give some'at to a pore h'old blind man, citizens—a chunk of bread, a bit o' meat, a sop o' wine . . ." But no one had given him any of these. "Give arf-an-obol to a weary h'old blind man, chaps . . . arf a happle, a b'iled hegg, a few nuts . . ." But no one had given him any of these things, either. Pappus did not bother even sighing. At least for the moment no one was pushing him aside, no one was tripping him up; it was not raining, and he was, in his niche, out of the wind. By and by he began to think that such a gathering as he was aware was going on, so far from the Sacred Precincts, must be rather odd. But he neither said nor did anything. Only, he listened. Always, in fact, he listened. It was surprising . . . or, it might have been surprising to others, if they had thought about it; it was not surprising to Pappus . . . how many, many people assumed, sans thought, that

because the old man was blind he must be deaf as
well. And he was not deaf. At all. Now and then
something was said in his near-presence which might
not have been said in the near-presence of another.
Often, of course, what this was which was so said
was either of no consequence or (to Pappus) of no
comprehension. Often. But not always. And sometimes he was able to repeat and to pass on what was
said to someone else. To whom it was of some consequence. Sometimes, an official. Sometimes, a private
person. And . . . sometimes . . . he was rewarded.

Never, of course, amply.

But even half a boiled egg is better than none.

Do not, in one way or another, most men and
most women sell their eyes?

Pappus sold his ears.

He did not now, anymore than ever, strain forward to listen. He never turned his head to listen; he
did not do so now.

Now and then he heard a shuffle. Now and then
he heard a step. Now and again he heard someone sit
. . . or, having sat a while, stand.

But one thing which he did not hear was a word.
Not in any idiom, accent, or tongue. Not one word.
To say that to Pappus, having spent so many, many
years being both blind and poor, to say that to him
many things must have happened which might be
described as *odd* would be to use a word for which
the rhetors have an especial term: let us however
merely call this, *understatement*. And yet what was
going on *now . . . here . . .* under the arches of what
had once been the Stoa . . . even to Pappus it seemed
odd. Aloud he said nothing. To himself he said, *Odd,
odd, damned, damned odd. Chaps might be so many*

*sleepwalkers . . . So they might . . . odd . . . damned
odd . . .*

"Well, well, and what's on next?" asked the
(*pro tem.* and *pro hac vice*) Reverend Sir Zosimus
Sulla of his equally—temporarily and for this occasion only—Reverend Brother.

Who answered, scanning the Bronze Tablets for
his cue, "Next? Next is . . . *'Sacrifice to Jupiter
Krapuvius . . .'* "

"Surely you're having me on? 'Jupiter
Kra*pu*vius'? Never *heard* of the chap—"

"Yes you have *too* heard of—"

"No I have *not*. Heard of the chap . . . ah, oh,
all honor to him all the same, hem, hem, *absit omen*
. . . Kra*pu*vius?"

"Should you prefer the alternate forms of
Krapouie, or *Crapouie*, with a *C*, or *Grabouie*, with a
G?"

"I should not."

"Well, *well*, then: *'Iuve Krapuvi*, a.k.a. Jove
and/or Jupiter Grabovius,' etc. etc.; told you a
several dozen *times* already!"

"Oh, very *well*, then, if you say so; alien deities
which our fathers knew not; naturalized into the
Pantheon by Decree of the Senate, I suppose; stan-
dard procedure. Very well, very well; pious Aeneas:
get along with it like a good chap, do."

They sacrificed to the local Jupiter with salt and
meal and fat; then they took off the wreaths of bay
leaves which they had just put on for the purpose:
this required them, of course, once again to pull their
togas partly up so as to cover the tops of their heads,
a measure eagerly resorted to by Sir Rufus Tiburnus,

who was as bald as a coot, and sensitive on the subject; but reluctantly followed by Sir Zosimus Sulla, who had trouble keeping the toga-fold from slipping down over his face altogether, which made him rather sullen: but they both did it.

"What's it say next?"

"Says, '*Pray in a murmur.*' Let us now pray in a murmur . . . Fact of the matter, old man," Sir Rufus murmured, "I can't *read* those lower lines at *all* . . . *Sun's* in the wrong direction; can *you* make anything out of it?"

Sir Zosimus seemed at first not to hear this question. Then he gave a very loud hiccup. Then his toga fell over his eyes once again. Then he suddenly got it clear, bent closer to the Bronzen Tablets, peered closely, and said, ". . . altogether in the wrong direction; no; not a thing. *Hujus, cujus, hic, haec, hunc!*" he suddenly announced in a quite loud voice, scattering meal with a sweeping gesture. The Plebs, who were dipping into the quite unexpected largesse of mead with utmost satisfaction, broke off to give very large cheers.

"*That's* the stuff," said Sir Rufus. "Good. Let's give 'em some more of the same. Er—*no!*"

"Why *not?*"

"Wrong *language*. Must have it all in *Um*brian. Otherwise: disaffection."

"Piffle. Except for the Quæstor, who dursn't come near us now, as we've frightened him half out of his wits, *none* of the people understand Umbrian anymore, it's utterly obsolete."

"Ah yes. *But they recognize the sound of it when they hear it . . .*"

"Hm. Yes. Quite. Well. What to do?"

"*Do?* Why, what one has just *done*. Only in

*Um*brian . . . you've not forgotten your paradigms, your declensions, your conjugations, *have* you?''

He stared at his Sacred Brother. His Sacred Brother stared back. ''I say, what an infernal impudence, one *never* forgets one's paradigms, declensions, and conjugations . . . Well, well. Onward, then.'' He cleared his throat loudly; this was perhaps a mistake, as at least a part of the crowd ceased chattering and tippling and began to look on with renewed interest.

Hastily, Sir Rufus launched into, ''*Hatu hahtu, mantraklu, mantrahklu, sate sahate, sahta sahata, eturstamu eheturstahamu . . .*''

And, as he paused for breath, Sir Zosimus chimed in with a responsive, ''*Meersta mersta!*''

''*Tekvias via arvia aviekla, purtuetu, ivekla . . .*''

''*Antentu atentu ustentu ustetu, krenkatru krikatru . . .*''

''*Anzeriatu azeriatu, onse uze.*''

''*Persnimu persnimu pesnimu pesnimu, persuntru pesnimu, persuntru persuntru pesuntru. Turse tuse—*''

''*Farsio fasio—*''

The assembly, from the Conscript Fathers to the Plebs, listened (and drank) with much satisfaction, as the familiar and utterly unintelligible (but: *familiar*) sounds of their sacred ancestral language rang through the air. Betimes first one and then the other of the visiting priests would flex or even kick a stiffening arm or leg (either motion being taken by the crowd for an hieratical gesture, or even perhaps the prescribed dance of the *tripudium*); and now and then, either out of sheer good spirits or perhaps a keen appetite one or both of the visiting priests would give a turn to the spits on which the sacrificial sows were slowly frizzling over their plats of glowing coals; and even the Quæstor—who was from time to time obliged to sample the golden mead by direction of the traditionally suspicious *gens Petronia* in order to demonstrate that it had not been poisoned—even the Quæstor nodded his head in satisfaction.

("Going very well, it seems, don't you think?" asked Sir T.)

("Going *very* well, it seems, don't you think?" said Sir Z.)

—And then, in, more or less, chorus—*"Haoinaf kapru kumpifiatu Krapuvi, tenzitum tuplak tuva* (numeral), *atru, testru* (initial *t*), *ustentu* (second *t*), *ententu, antentu, ampentu* (orthographical variant) . . . *Krapuvi, kumiaf . . ."*

("I say, I had forgotten that I remembered so much of it) . . . *krenkratum krikatru* (second *k*), *Ikuvins, iveka . . ."*

("I say, so had *I*: beastly dialect I used to think it, brings back old times, m' pædagogue used to flog me if I got a single syllable wrong, poor dear old chap, what comes next?"

And, off under the west portico of what used to be the Stoa, the ones summoned and sent thither by one whose life was but a dream but whose dreams directed many and many a life, these having within them an order which said that no sword should be swung until the ritual salt be flung into the fires—these slouched sullenly, shivered sometimes, scowled somewhat . . . now and then . . . or, more often, looked nowhere in particular: and there, only blankly—and waited—

—and waited—

* * *

Although the road Peregrine was now on must almost certainly have been one of the narrowest roads ever built by any Imperial Corps of Engineers—and, absolutely certainly, one of the last—it was in every wise other than width a typical Roman road: and ran straight as a line in a geometry, as far as Peregrine could see. He suddenly wished that he could see a lot farther. He wished now, very much, that he had taken thought to climb a tree, at least *one* tree, how could he have been so stupid as not to have done so?—back where there had *been* trees—in order to scout and spy and peer for his Alvish friends . . . or else (he now wished, while he was wishing) that he'd asked the dryad-haunted trees themselves to do so for him. But, as is almost always the case, all the wishes in the world would not now do what he himself had left undone.

Some slight mounds and low hillocks, which alone broke the level monotony of the land, he now observed to be the overgrown ruins of the larger buildings of what had clearly been a much larger place of habitation, ere Roma's woes began: the present hamlet seemed to lie entirely within what was once the Agora . . . and, to a very limited extent still was, if the two old women selling withered parsnips and carrots and the one old man offering wine from one jar and oil from another (very bad wine and very bad oil, by the smell of them) could be said to make a market-place . . .

Huts had been reared up out of rubble and thatch, somewhat sturdier structures out of reclaimed brick; but the center of the place was an architectural melange which would have given Vitruvius mad dreams: mismatched pillars dragged from sundry temples built in sundry centuries in sundry styles, ashlars smooth and ashlars rough (the spaces between them chinked with bad plaster covering worse mortar), and the whole, with its few clustering outbuildings tiled with an infinite variety of tiles, some broken, some merely cracked, many covered with moss which concealed who-knewethwhat . . .

And, by virtue of such exemplary designs and symbolic insignia as: a fish . . . a *Chi Rho* . . . a serpent bearing a crown with a cross upon it . . . several items of old marble statuary of the male sex placed upside down in lieu of other masonry, each one with its nose and penis carefully smashed off . . . Peregrine knew that what he was seeing (as he plodded in on Dobbin, or whatever the quadruped's name) was the local heretical church.

If not indeed the local heretical cathedral.

Indeed, many a cathedral in those days was considerably smaller—not that this church was particularly *large*—but it was, after all, merely: a church. Father Fufluns had done everything he could think of to have it consecrated a cathedral; he had had it declared a basilica (and everyone knew that a basilica was entitled to become a cathedral); he had held bazaars until its mortgage had been paid off; he had, and at no small cost, managed to have the hamlet elevated to the status of a city: all for nought: were it have been made a cathedral, the next step would inescapably have been for Father Fufluns to have been made a bishop.

And, faced with this necessity, the hierarchy of the Neognostic Heterodox Heretical Church, although known far and wide for its liberal, not to say, latitudinarian, attitude, had unexpectedly (or, perhaps, expectedly) proved coy.

So it remained a *church*.

Lounging around outside and evidently waiting for the service to begin, was what Perry supposed must be the congregation, and a rather scanty congregation it was; and as for its members, many of them bore the almost certain signs of the rather dottier heresies (as distinct from the fine, fierce, fanaticism of the major denominations), such as the look of having been knocked about the head with a whippletree, a sort of miracle in itself, inasmuch as the whippletree had yet to be invented (but in many a cellar many an inventor with lean limbs and lank hair bent over his vice and lathe and bench; did the neighbors enquire—and they *did*—What did he be a-doin? the answer was, oft as not, He be a-inventin of the whippletree!—whereat great was the laughter of the scornful): but be all that as it may.

Perry dismounted, tied his horse to the stump of what had once been a pillar (though whether Doric, Corinthian, or Iambic Pentameter, not enough remained to say) in a temple of an Abomination, found a very small coin in the corner of his purse, purchased a bunch of well-ripened carrots and fed it to the beast; then wandered over to listen to the talk outside the portico. As a birthright Pagan, he had grown up in a religion without very much talk to it (nor, for that matter, very much action), and the ever-ready readiness of Christians to talk about their own religion . . . and to talk and *talk* and TALK . . . always fascinated him. Two of the dottykinses were at it already. He listened.

"What, don't they do Imbibulation where you comes from?" one such asked the other such. His accents were those of Babylonia Philadelphia . . . or, perhaps, of Alexandria Philadelphia, Seleucia Philadelphia, Ptolemy Philadelphia, or any one other of the twenty-seven or thirty-seven cities of the Graeco-Roman world, all named, in one way or another, *Philadelphia*: *God* knows why: the foundation for jokes about Philadelphia had already been well-laid.

"Nao, they daon't, and a man could die o' thirst as a result, an full hundred parasangs I've come for it, for a pilrinage, as ye might say; and naow they tell me *this* priest fellow here, *he* daon't dew it neither," said the other.

"Well, don't be in a snit and a haste; for one thing, you gets the plenary indulgency for the pilrinage alone; then, too, maybe he *do* do it."

The lean, dehydrated features of the other one lit up. "Ayo, yew think sao?"

The Philadelphian hedged slightly. "Well, I dunno for sure, but no harm in asking; he do levi*ta*tion—"

'Ayo, he *dew*? Well, well, then—"

The Philadelphian hedged again. He might have been a lawyer. "Uh, well, only on movable feasts to be sure."

"Well, that be nao problem. Today must be a movable feast, for look at that there sacristan a-movin' o' the victuals from the kitching tew the parsonage right naow. Sao he *be*. Well, naow? I've brought my own water, and if he *dew* dew Imbibulation, he'll change it inter wine . . ."

Something struck a note in Perry's mind; he was by no means sure what the evidently heretical Sacrament of Levitation involved, but—

A portly, late-middle-aged man now approached and asked him, "And what are *you* here for, young fellow?"

Peregrine thought it best to tell at least part of the truth. "Levitation," he said.

'So'm I,'' said the citizen, gazing at Perry with a calculating eye. ''What's *your* reason?—youthful indiscretions, I suppose?''

'' 'There is nothing indiscreet about them, he replied stiffly,' '' said Perry, having his own little joke.

"Well, wait till you get my age," said the grizzling; "if you want to talk about nothing stiffly . . . well, Levitation may be heretical, some say it is, but what *I* say, *I* say it jiggles you and joggles you and it lifts you up—'*up*,' get what I mean?—and it starts all the benign humours flowing and it lets them overflow according to their natural pattern; know what I mean?" And he nudged Perry with a portly, middle-aged elbow.

"I do indeed," said Peregrine, this time with less of a joke. His own benign humours had been flowing and overflowing without feminine accompaniment far too often of late, according to their natural patterns or otherwise; and, reminded of this matter yet again, he gazed round about in hopes of sight of one of those Christian virgins who (as oft he had been told), defying Pagan overtures, preferred death to dishonor; only maybe not: he could not see a one: at least not a one under some such immense age as perhaps fifty, virgin or otherwise.

So who cared.

And then, next, somehow so swiftly that he was afterwards not able to explain exactly how, he found himself confronting a man in semi-clerical costume (to wit, Basnobio), being relieved by him of one small gold and one large silver coin; of being firmly if gently moved to a certain spot upon a certain tessellated pavement and told, "Stand here. And, whenever you hear me snap my fingers once: *bow*." And when I snap 'em twice, *kneel*." There was an altar. There was a priest. There was no backing out, *now*.

The priest took up in his hands two fans made of eagles' feathers and and he bowed low before the altar and began to pray. Basnobio approached, bowed, set a thurible of smoking incense before him, bowed again, and withdrew. From the sidelines he snapped his fingers, *once*. Peregrine bowed; *twice*, Peregrine knelt. The priest continued to say his prayers in a low incessant voice and by and by he began with gentle movements to fan the incense; and, as the volume of the sacred scented smoke increased, he passed the fans through it . . . once . . . twice . . . thrice . . . Then he turned and faced Peregrine, kneeling with bowed head before him.

"O Thou Who didst bear the Children of Israel as on eagles' wings," intoned Father Fufluns, "and Who didst deny even unto Solomon knowledge of the way of the eagle in the midst of the air, do Thou, O Ancient of Days and Ruler of the Realms of Air, be pleased to make known unto this Thy child here reverently bowing down before Thee in the manner of Cherubim and Seraphim; Thou Who didst fly upon the wings of the Cherub—"

Faintly, Peregrine, deeply moved in spite of all, heard as though from a distance the sound of something between a hiss and a squawk; which he attributed—inasmuch as he attributed it to anything—to aspects of the clamorous denunciations with which one sect of this most multisectarian of religions were wont betimes to afflict upon another: certainly there seemed to be a note of derision: but he returned his thoughts in concentration upon the ceremony: meanwhile the lips of Father Fufluns (crazy, mazy, and dazy he might have been: faithless he was not) were seen to move regardless of the interruption.

"—the Seraph of six wings and with twain he did fly, as revealed to the eye of Thy Prophet—"

Hissssss!

Squawwwk!

"—administer with plenary grace this sacred Sacrament of Levitation unto Thy servant," here Father Fufluns waved the fans of eagles' feathers over Peregrine's head with a slow and singular motion upward, as one who with great dignity invites others to get off of the grass—

Peregrine began to feel an absolute compulsion, he could not say why, to stand on his toes . . . Incredulous, and yet acceptant, he observed the ground give way beneath him . . . His limbs, which had been in the kneeling posture, straightened; he rose until his eyes were level with the downcast eyes of Fufluns the Priest, then with the top of the priest's head, then he looked down upon the tonsure (this, too, was heretical, being square in shape, doubtless the influence of the Varangian Guard), then he had to bend a bit to see the priest at all, then he ceased to look down at all: and still . . . slowly, slowly, slowly . . . he rose, and rose, and *rose* . . .

. . . down below, an increasingly faint voice was heard to intone, ". . . flights of Seraphs and flights of Angels, world without end, forever and ever, Aeons like Angels, Demiurge and Demigorgon . . ." Father Fufluns had slipped over once again into unforgivable old Gnosticims: but of course Peregrine did not know; and if he did, he would not have cared.

What he *did* care was about a damned good scan of the *land*: and afar off, to the North, whence Boreas eeke with his rude breath, etc. etc., he saw or he *thought* he saw a line of trees winding their way along the flatness of that flatmost land, and he knew this must indicate a river or anyway a stream . . . in other words: *water*: requisite for women, men, and beasts alike, since e'en kings and queens must live by nature; plus a small what-was-it? . . . too low-staying to be a puff of smoke, so likelier was a cloud of dust . . . just . . . perhaps just large enough to indicate a group and troop of people of the size he was seeking after, to wit his friends the Alves: and just as he was straining for a better look he felt himself sinking.

"Hey down there, Reverend Father," he called through cupped hands, "can't you keep me up here a while longer?"

The voice of the priest, as it rose thinly through the air, was tinged, perhaps, less with mysticism than with mere annoyance. "Charismatic chiropractic, boy!" he exclaimed. "Do you take me for a mage or a thaumaturge? I can't perform miracles: down you come as down you must . . ." But although Peregrine did not rise any higher, neither did he sink any lower; and, the congregation evidently commenting on this phenomenon, the priest by and by looked up. His mouth fell awry and a-gape. Had Perry been a bit closer he might have observed the man swallow. After a moment the priest called up, cupping his own hands, "Have you received Christian Baptism in any form whatsoever, Orthodox, Unorthodox, Heterodox, Heretical, Schismatic, Charismatic, Valid, Invalid, Conditional, Unconditional, Clandestine, or even merely Irregular?" Peregrine thought it best not to answer. "You *have*n't, *have* you, you foolish fellow; well, then, you see what happens: the Sacrament of Levitation in your case is not merely voidable, but *void*. And I wash my hands of it,'' and here he lightly dipped his digits into a small finger-bowl provided for the purpose.

The Neognostic Heterodox Heretical Church thought of almost everything.

What was left of the congregation by this time (a part of it had already fled) uttered sundry small anathemas (major anathemas, as was well-known, could be issued only by members of the episcopate or by lower clergy under special episcopal license), made the sign of the cross in every conceivable manner, and in some few cases stooped to pick pebbles which they tossed up as a sort of surrogate stoning (indeed, only fairly recently, a sect in Syria had advanced the doctrine that stoning itself might be considered in itself a Sacrament; but they had all been stoned); these congregants may or may not have heard of the law of gravity under that or any other name, but there were, very, very shortly, irritated little yelps, in various regional accents, of, ''Dawn't play the fool, now, I a'n't no fooking eretic, bounce another o' them ahf me pate and I'll have at yez, see if I dawn't;'' and very similar disaffected outcries.

Father Fufluns himself had vanished by now, after having declared the administration of Sacramental Levitation under Suspension until further notice; and his deacon, subdeacon, and acolyte (actually all three offices were held by his assistant, Basnobio, as the practice of Plurality had not yet been officially condemned; though there were rumors it would be taken up at the next General Council, as soon as they had finished with unfinished business, one almost perpetual item of which was the perpetually dubious

Doctrine of Caesaropapism, a perennially touchy
subject, and one which the current Great White
Caesar had been cutting up rough about, threatening
to impale the Fathers and Doctors and other Coun-
cilmen wholesale if they so much as touched upon it)
were—or, to be precise, *was*—dismantling the altar.

"Hey down there! Hey! Hey, I say!" cried
Peregrine, shouting down. Basnobio looked up,
enquiringly. "Hey, what am I going to *do*?" cried
Peregrine.

Basnobio was seldom at a loss for words, that is,
Basnobio was seldom at a loss for certain words.
"Got any *money*?" he called up.

Perry patted his pouch. "Not an obol," he said.

Basnobio sighed a sigh of genuinely sincere
regret. "Then even simony wouldn't help," he answered.

"What am I going to *do*?"

"That's *your* problem," said the fellow, getting
on with his work; then, a mote of humor floating
into his mind, with slight upward canting of his head,
added "You might, if you were *any* kind of a Christian, pray for an angel, *haw*!"; and, without award-
ing the jest the merit of even a second *haw*, started
off with his sacred burden into the sacred precincts.

Peregrine, who had gradually and uneasily become aware of rising winds, thought the winds were
tossing words around; or was there an echo? Certainly he heard the words "*An angel! An angel!*" being repeated . . . shouted . . . screamed . . . by those
who still stayed in view on the grounds below . . . saw
Father Fufluns thrust his head out of the parsonage
window and hastily withdraw it, saw the head of
Basnobio appear in the same place, instantly vanish,
saw and heard the window being slammed shut, and

bolted . . . he saw, Peregrine, a shadow the most strange, and he heard—he was sure he heard—the beating of mighty wings. "Idiots, *that is no angel!*" one voice he clearly heard, which he thought might be that of the portly middle-aged man with the querulous prostate or whatever associated problems. "*That is a———*"

The winds and other sounds swept the man's words away; one of the other sounds being of course that of the beating of mighty wings, and another sounded, and most oddly, like a cry of, "*Ballast! Ballast, ahoy!*"

Perry smelt something very much like a fish dinner in rather early stages of preparation, and something mighty strong took hold of him on each side, but in no way painfully, something . . . some-*things* . . . folded deftly under each of his arms, and a rather familiar voice said, almost, if not quite, in his ears, "Well, me little biped, and aren't you one of old Alf's straggle and stirpes?

Perry dared look up. "*Smarasderagd!*" he cried.

"That same," said that same. "Have you anything to fix, have you anything to mend, have you any little tricks to which a dragon might attend?"

After some while, things in the hamlet returned to something like order. (The hamlet, after sufficient fiscal persuasion, had not merely been restored by the Imperial Authorities to full municipal status, it had been full renamed by them as *Caesarea Augusta Philadelphia*, and, considering that the Barbarians had called it something like *Glopz*, who could really blame the Imperial Authorities?) The priest and his assistant had climbed out from under the bed, and were now discussing recent events.

"That was certainly The Great Red Dragon and the Woman Clothed With The Sun," said Father Fufluns, bolting his tiffin.

"That was certainly nothing of the sort," said Basnobio, a stiff-necked fellow if ever was.

"That was certainly The—"

"The dragon was not red and there was no woman clothed with the sun . . . or, for that matter, with anything else . . ."

"It *was*n't? She *was*n't?" The face of Father Fufluns became considerably brighter. "Well! Be that as it may, it reminds me of. my many other pastoral duties, toil toil toil, morning to night, a layman works from sun to sun but a cleric's work is never done: unclothing the naked, my plain and bounden duty, see the Pistis Sophia, Editio Maioram (or is it Marjoram?), Revised and Reorganized and Reoriented, Second Rescension with Illustrations, XII, 12–25 . . ."

And by this time, for he could put on considerable speed when requisite, he was facing the door of a rather small house on the outskirts of town: which is to say, on the other side of the former Agora: *Knock-knock!*

"Who's there?"

"Father Fufluns, and how is my little pigeon today?"

"Oh Popsy I feel so . . . so . . . I jist dunno howda describe it," said a female voice, somewhat whiney to be sure, but *A whiney wench is better to no wench a-tall*, as they have it in the Varangian, the Visogothic, and a mickle many other dialects; in he went; "Are you properly clothed under them broidered sheets, my daughter?"

"Course I am, whatcher fink?"

"Well, then, I'll unclothe you . . . and next we'll see about visiting you, another of my bounden duties, let them say what they like, *'Set a lion on Fufluns,'* or whatever they like to say . . . no, no, ha ha, fool that I am, I *am* visiting you. Well, let me get these robes off, canonically and otherwise superfluous for the purpose to hand, are my hands cold? well, we'll warm them, then, won't we? . . . what would be next, *oh* yes: next thing is to let me see about casting out dæmons!"

Several score dæmons, who had been lazying around, pricked up their batlike little ears at this, and began a squeaking chorus of, "Oh for pity's sake do let a dæmon *be* for once and a change, carntcher?" and, "Bugger me sidewise, it's that old womanizer and wowser Fufluns once again!" and, "Dirty old chap, if there's anything I can't stand it's a dirty old chap," and, "Oh I say look oh how disgusting, out of here at once is where I'm going, my mam didn't whelp me to witness scenes such as yon there below; fie!" "And fee and fo and fum!" . . . in a moment more the dæmons, utterly cast out, were blearily blinking their weeny rufous eyes in the bright light of the out-of-doors and rather sullenly flapping their wings and drifting down-wind looking for someone or something else to go and possess, even as it might be an herd of swine; though even there, as one or two darkly remarked, one could no longer be sure . . .

Smarasderagd was not in the least bit hostile, nor was he, he made it clear, in the least whit willing to risk himself by taking Perry to anyplace where Perry wanted to go: and of course, Perry at the moment wanted only to go wherever his friends King

Alf and Prince Buck might be . . . wherever that might be . . . "Precious fool I should be going *there*, wherever *there* may be, where *they* are, I mean . . . until, anyway, they become used to the changed order of events, that is: so there!"

"*Which* changed order of events?"

"The order of events intendant upon the roaring flames of the dragons' revolution," was the answer, with a touch of reproof; and at this the dragon issued forth a whoosh of breath and flame: ending on a slightly fishy belch, and the words, "See what I mean?"

"Oh yes, you mean that henceforth you are keeping the treasures and they can be keeping the trash fish," Peregrine said, recollecting what had occurred back at Alf Big House; namely the curious incident whence had come the flight of himself, his friends, and all, what time Smarasderagd had played for keeps that which previously had been little more than a game.

"Ex*act*ly," said Smarasderagd.

"Where *will* you take me, then?"

But the dragon implied that this question was wrongly couched. "I am not 'taking you' anywhere," said he. "*I* am going where *I* am going, which is nowhere dependent upon where *you* want to go, and *you* are not going as a passenger; you are coming along as *bal*last, a fact which you will simply have to accept . . . Drat these winds . . . *Eh* . . . ?"

Inasmuch as Perry had not asked a further question, he had no answer to supply to the *"Eh?"* He saw something long and black and bifurcated shoot forth and wobble. This was several times repeated, and he realized that it was Smarasderagd's tongue which he was seeing; then, once again, Smarasderagd said, "*Eh!*"—but this time it was no question. The dragon seemed puzzled; the dragon seemed displeased. "*Drat!*" said the dragon. And hissed some susurration, sibilant of surprise and of displeasure.

"Hadn't heard that in *years!*" said the dragon, as though to himself. "What can it mean?"

Peregrine did not feel able to answer anymore this time than the last; he could wonder at the dragon's wonder, but he could do no more. However, as he watched their shadows on the earth beneath, he did become aware of something on which he felt he might certainly comment. "Aren't we changing directions?" he asked.

"Of *course* we're changing directions! We *must*! And insomuch as we must, off we go, as go we must, little though any of this may please you, my little Christian."

"Who, *me*?"

Plains, hills, dales, vales, here and some strips of plowland.

"Yes, *you*.—why? Do you notice anyone else up here with us?"

Smarasderagd had for long been holding Perry's whole body more or less horizontally and with all four limbs. The notion of speaking impertinently to a dragon was not one which would have naturally occurred to him . . . Smarasderagd was after all only the second dragon he had ever seen in his whole life and this was only the second time he had ever seen Smarasderagd . . . and, certainly, at this height, sarcasm, even irony, was not to be thought of. Smarasderagd might certainly be, as King Alf had asserted, piscivorous: But he need, after all, not *eat* Perry.

He need only drop him.

"Compared to your own dragonic greatness," he said, choosing his words with care; "I am certainly little. But I am not a Christian."

"Well now, I must say, you do speak nice. —you're *not*?"

"No, I'm not."

A small silence. "I used to have some very nice Jewish friends," the dragon said.

What *did* Peregrine believe? He thought aloud. "My old father used to say, 'The gods—which is to say an allegorical expression of the infinite attributes of the First Cause—' "

"Well, *that*'s nice, too . . . Who's your father?"

Perry said, "He's called King Palindrome, but his name is actually King Paladrine, and he is, actually, the last Pagan king in Lower Europe."

At the word "king" Smarasderagd went very slightly stiff. Then asked, "He doesn't play tricks with *dragons*, does he?"

"No, never. Poor sweet old fellow. I hope all's well with him."

He felt Smarasderagd relax; the dragon did not at once reply; it might have seemed that he was turning something over in his mind. Then he said, "Well . . . I suppose as we must do this, we might as well do this in style . . . I can't go down. Not now. Not just yet. So we must do something in the middle of the air, but don't be frightened, now, do you *hear*?"

Perry heard. And asked, "Do what? Frightened of what?"

"*You*'ll see. Just don't struggle, is all."

Peregrine, in what followed, strove hard to keep all this in mind, and, fortunately, he succeeded.

"*Mers, teitu, nurpener, sumel, rufru* (I've always detested these irregular verbs) . . ."

"(Sshh, these aren't verbs.)"

"(Don't you sshh me; well, I've always detested them anyway.)"

Together: "*Aterafust ahatripursatu ahtrepuratu, arpes arepes tertu titu!*"

From the seats round about the one side of the sacred precincts where the seats had not fallen in, one of the Conscript Fathers observed, at large, "Well, one must declare that these visiting priests do speak the Old Language uncommonly well."

And behind him, one of the Plebs said, "Ah, there ain't nothink like a eddication; my old gaffer, *he could write his own name!* And many's the time he says to me, 'Bobus,' says he, 'when I puts my sig*nay*ture on a dockyment, there can't be no con*trove*rsy'!"

Sir Zosimus, breaking into Latin: ". . . '*gh* normally becomes h *h* initially and medially, cf. Oscan *ee-hiianasúm.*"

"(Psst: I don't think that part comes in to this part.)"

"(I should think not, too.)"

"(Well, why did you *say* it, then?)"

"Because it's so *absurd*, *that's* why: *ee-hiianasum*, indeed! Hee-hee!)"

"(Jove! I believe that you are tiddly, my Learned Brother!)"

"(Fine one to talk; I believe that you are tiddly, too, my Burnèd Lover!)"

Overcome with laughter, the two old priests *pro*

tem. fell into one another's arms and lurched and staggered round about, narrowly escaping falling into the barbecue pits. Sir Zosimus, having barked his shin, held on to his fellow as he hopped about on one leg.

A Pleb.: "What be they a-doin' of *now*?"

A Conscript Father: "Dancing the *tripudium*, as is requisite, of course."

The wind shifted, bringing the sacred smell of roasting sacrifical pig to the seats, and producing once again a well-nigh universal murmur of, "It's that Old Time Religion, and it's good enough for me!"

As Sir Rufus and Sir Zosimus paused for breath, the Quæstor approached with a manner mingled of dignity and caution, bowed gravely to both of them, gravely turned one of the Bronze Tablets around, bowed again, and a few steps withdrew.

The two consulted.

"What's all this about?"

"Dunno. Best have a look . . . Ah. He thinks we've finished up that side of the Tablet, so he's turned it round so we can finish up the other side as well. Hmmm. Oh! Jolly good! The letters on this side are *much* larger!"

"Oh I say what a blessing. Those blasted paradigms were getting to me . . . What's it say? Ah. Says, *The Senior Brother*, or 'Brother-Superior,' distinction without a difference, *now sounds the* Summons *and then the General Assembly*; who's the Brother-Superior, I forget—"

"*I* am."

"Oh. I thought *you* were."

"I *am*—"

"Well, then, get *on* with it, 'stead of just stand-

ing there like a crane on one foot . . . I say, *no*, it is *I*
who am standing here like a crane on one foot.
Oh well. *Tch!*"

The Quæstor now announced, as loudly as
possible, "Pray, silence, Citizens of New Iguvium in
Nova Umbria! Pray, silence, whilst Their Holinesses
the Most Reverend and Right Reverend the Aetidian
Brothers pronounce the Summons! Augurs, man
your staffs! Clean quarterings, port and starboard,
fore and aft!"

It was—or was about to be—a great moment for
the augurs, for their collective status, once very high,
had, under Christian proscription, fallen very low indeed; indeed, for some time now, instead of publicly
and honorably reading the auspices and omens on
which the welfare of State and City might well
depend, they had for the most part and in order to
keep body and soul together, been reduced to reading
palms, giving advice to the lovelorn, and, in some
several sad instances, even to sweeping crossings, or
peddling hot-cakes from door to door: it was damnably difficult keeping them hot, and, in fact, they
usually did not sell very well at all. As a result, the
characters of one or two of the augurs had been
perhaps somewhat corrupted: one such was even to
be heard, in a mutter which others pretended not to
hear, clandestinely observing the weather (". . .
strong headwinds from north northwest . . .") before
the actual sounding of the Summons: which was not
the thing at all, very bad form, and enough to have
softened the hard heart even of Cato the Elder,
whose coarse comment that "He did not understand
how two augurs could pass each other without burst-
ing out laughing," had never been forgiven by them:
and never would.

But the Summons had already begun, and was
even now *"summoning birds which fly* [no one
would, after all, summon an *ostrich*], *winged
creatures which fly, to fly from the east, to fly from
the south, from the west, from the north, from and
to the right and left; to provide omens, to supply
auspices, wisdom, counsel, guidance and advice: we
summon you: we summon you: we summon you:
may your presences be favorable. We adjure, conjure, compel you; hearken, therefore, and
appear . . ."*

And, in the ringing silence which followed, Sir
Rufus breathed into Sir Zosimus's ear, "Awesome
powers, these." Sir Zosimus nodded.

But neither one really understood just how
awesome those powers really were.

The only maps with much pretense to accuracy
or precision in the matter of exact boundaries were
cadastral maps: it was certainly essential to know
where one ward or one municipium began, began and
left off, that is, if one expected to collect taxes and
not arguments; hence such details as ". . . *and from
the grey dovecote to the blasted oak, and thence at a
line constituting the brook called* . . ." Well,
whatever . . . The boundaries between nations were
designated in theory by such things as mountains and
deserts, though in practice much likelier by battles.
Immense battles had been fought, and with immense
losses of lives, to be commemorated with immense
monumental inscriptions (some of these illustrated in
great and ghastly detail): but nowadays very often
the scenes of such triumphs—if that is what they may
rightfully be called—were observed chiefly by the
hedgehog and the owl, to whom the matter of how

many heads, hands, feet, noses, and genitalia had been severed was probably one of great indifference.

Since the division and redivision of the Roman Empire; the incursions of the Barbarians; the civil wars and the wars between the states, the rival generals, emperors, and caesars; the religious persecutions; and all the rest of it—since all this had begun, and still continued to continue, the matter of what boundaries lay where and who ruled over which was not so certain as it had once been, and the idea that it might soon (or ever) be once for all resolved was not one which found ready acceptance. Baron Bruno, for example, a man who was not often perplexed, was not only not certain that he was still in his own High King's domains and dominions, he was no longer exactly certain where he was at all. He kept his eyes always open, but the fact now was that his eyes were growing heavier and heavier. He was not even aware when they closed.

He and his two cavalrymen and three foot-sloggers might well, once they entered into the circle of rune-thorns, have walked themselves, widdershins, to death, without once waking up to observe the fact. They were, in fact, "*where no ass brayed, and no cock crew*"—a place most dangerous to be, as dangerous as cold iron; it was unknown to them that, a good league thence, and (as it were) underneath a mountain, one solitary smallholder managed still to till his few strips of grainland, cultivate his small truck garden, prune his grove of trees and press himself enough oil and wine for his own needs. There was nothing idyllic or arcadian about this life, the labor was immense, wolves and bears had begun to appear—but—and this was his greater fortune—in many years: no *soldiers*. His greater infortune was to

have met a boar whilst he went to fetch water; the
boar ripped him from knee to navel, and after that
his luck, like his lifeblood, ran out very quickly.

The wolves ate his sheep and goats, and the
foxes and the weasels got most of his hens. The cock
flew up first into one tree and then into another and
thence into another, and another; and the ass simply
wandered away, browsing upon the tough thistle and
the tender grass alike; the feral dog which thought to
bring him down was driven off with flying hooves
and rib-cracking kicks. There was no particular
reason *why* the cock and the ass should have gone in
the direction they both did, though by different ways
and at different speeds, save perhaps that this way,
lying down-slope, was easier to follow. That either
one ever actually reached the old road, and what happened to them afterwards, did they or did they not,
does not matter: it matters only that, within hearing of a certain place upon that old road, the cock
crew . . . and the ass brayed . . .

And that, of course, broke the charm. And the
spell.

The Baron and his men, much though they had
slept the whilst they walked in circles, were obliged to
sleep e'en more, by reason of their great fatigue.

And after that, went on.

Whither they went, they knew not; the men
would have by all or any means returned, but to gain-
say Baron Bruno was not possible, and he held no
councils of war. Or of any other kind. Two faces
danced always before his red, red, swollen eyes, were
his eyes now open or closed: one was a face even
uglier than his own, and it snarled and growled at
him, saying, *What! You are still 'ere? Harms! Orse!
Presue! Fetch! Begorn!* and the other face was

nothing ugly at all, the other face was damnably comely, and this other face said no word to him, he saw it only in profile, but when he saw it—and he saw it half of always—another voice spoke when he saw this other face, perhaps there had once been two such voices, both of women . . . young women . . . but now they were but one voice. Saying, *That is him . . . Peregrine . . .*

Meanwhile, Gaspar the Dreamer dreamed his dreams . . . which is to say, being Gaspar the Dreamer, he dreamed the dreams of other folk . . . and dreamed them for them . . . And, often . . . very, very often . . . that which he dreamed, did come to pass. But (as we may have said before; and if so, we say it again; and if not, we say it now) dreams are unlike propositions in geometry, although they may be fully as true; although they may be fully as true, they may not be measured, they may not be demonstrated: sometimes the parallel lines of dreams meet in infinity. And sometimes they do not meet at all.

Assassins waited for Peregrine. Soldiers pursued him. A petty king and a petty court, dismayed, wished he were with them. A princess missed him. It was of course true that she was a young, a very young princess. She knew little of the greater world and almost nothing of its events. But, what she knew, she knew. The mimworms had not lied to her nor to her sister. "It all be that dragon," she whispered. And her sister whispered back, "It be. It be."

Sir Zosimus Sulla was fretful. "Me voice is almost gone," he croaked. "I couldn't read another line of Umbrian just now to save me life. Me foot still hurts where I bumped it, then. And no birds are coming. Not so far as I can see. Or hear. So what shall we *do*?''

Sir Rufus Tiburnus was almost as played out, but he had the benefits of a military career, and as, as any good military commander—any good Pagan one, that is—he had had practical experience with the matter of recalcitrant birds of omen. ''When in doubt, scatter grain,'' he said. ''Where *is* the grain? Ah. On *your* side. Your pidjin, then. Scatter *grain*, I say.''

Grain was scattered.

''The augurs will simply go *mad*,'' said Sir Rufus, rubbing his gouty old hand. He seemed to look forward to this. Well, it had been a trying day, a *very* trying day. And it was not yet over.

The birds, on seeing the grain being scattered . . . and not all of them were far-sighted, but those who weren't of course observed the movements of those who were . . . at once began to fly towards the sacred precincts, and, in a moment, the middle upper air was filled with their cries.

''Crikey! Crikey! Corn, corn, corn!''

''Psst! Psst! Seed! Seed, seed, seed! Spelt, spelt, spelt!''

''Bugs? Bugs? Bug-bug-bug-a-bug-bug-bug-bug!''

Instantly, and exactly as prophesied by Sir R. Tiburnus, the augurs *did* go mad—or seemed to—and, in defiance of the traditional rule of strict silence whilst the omens were being taken, as traditionally broke the strict silence, and rushed from their seats with eager cries of, ''*Ibs*, I observe a starling in the west, a crow in the west! A wood-pecker in the east!'' and, ''*Dibs, I* observe a wood-

pecker in the east, a magpie in the east! Divine
messengers! *Dibs, dibs*!''

''*Dibs! Dibs! Dibs!*''

One of the augurs, Cassandros by name, who
had always been considered, well, a little bit *odd*,
said nothing whatsoever, but continued staring, with
one hand shading his eyes; no one paid *him* any
mind.

And, of course, every augur carried a special
staff with the aid of which he took his bearings; it
was of the utmost importance not only to observe the
kind and the number of birds (for every schoolboy
knows the story about Romulus and Remus and the
vultures), but from which quarter of the heavens they
appeared: thus, the staff. And, as the birds came
flocking in, all the augurs began waving their staffs
and then holding them up to quarter the heavens,
bumping into one another, commencing elaborate
apologies, breaking them off to take fresh auspices.
It was quite a spectacle; a show, in short, every bit as
interesting as the one which the visiting priests had
been putting on, and it was just as well so many birds
had (with some small assistance) appeared to answer
the Summons, for the sacrificial swine were not yet
entirely cooked: and the populus, with idle time on
its collective hands, might else have chosen to ex-
ersize its quasi-traditional right to riot.

And now one of the augurs, whose eyesight was
perhaps not equal to his enthusiasm, cried, ''*Dibs* I
see an hoopoe in the middle-west!''

Now, everyone knew about starlings, crows,
woodpeckers, and magpies; such birds were seen
even when no official auspices were being taken . . .
but—*a hoopoe?*

''Well, I snum!'' exclaimed one of the Conscript

Fathers. "I haven't heard of a hoopoe being observed since the Consulate of . . . of . . . name's on the tip of my tongue: *Caligula's horse?*"

Excitement is always contagious; many of the Plebs took up the subject with shouts of "A 'oopoe! A 'oopoe! Why, us 'asn't never *seed* no 'oopoe!"

In little more than a moment the rumor had swept a part of the throng that a *hippo* had been seen in the middle-west: the effect of this was tremendous; it affected even the few Christians who had been lurking round about, and, having been solemnly warned by their bishops that the eye which so much as *looked* willingly upon a Pagan ceremony would go blind, were observed now and then furtively peeping with one hand over one eye . . . just in case. "A hippo?" cried one such to another. "Surely it be the beast Behemoth of the Book of Job!"

"Nay, mayhap it be the Beast of the Apocalypse!"

Such distinctions did not affect the citizenry; if there were—and had not many of them just that moment *heard* there were—a hippo anywhere around, that same many damned well intended to see it! *Where was it?* And, as the augur who had thought he had espied a hoopoe, or a*n* hoopoe, in the middle-west, ran wildly in that direction waving his augurial staff, he was of course followed by lots and lots of other augurs, jealous of such an auspicious (or, as it might prove to be, *in*auspicious) sighting: waving *their* augurial staffs: the mob followed the augurs.

The augur who had gotten the head start ran at full speed, closely followed by many of his fellows, directly along the west wing of the Stoa.

Where, as we have seen, there waited a several

sundry men of sullen slumber: though now, as it were, full-wide-awake. And armed.

Meanwhile, and as the rest of the augurs who had stayed behind, gathered together, chattering like so many birds themselves, to tot up their totals and calculate their quarterings and consult their official standards and their personal notebooks—all, of course, with the intention of arriving at a concensus of *what it all really meant*—the augur Cassandros did not join them in this, and, instead, continued to gaze . . . and then to mumble . . . and then (his voice was old but his voice was strong) to declare what he himself was sighting, to wit:

"In the east, divine messengers!"

"Well, let's see, now, three starlings, four crows, eleven woodpeckers: now, that makes—"

"Beg pardon, but inasmuch as I myself *clearly* sighted no less than *six* starlings—"

"Double vision, that's what you've got."

"Well, I simply beg your pardon, I do *not* have double vision, and so—"

"In the east, divine messengers!"

". . . and four magpies in the south . . ."

"*In the east, divine messengers!*"

The other augurs paused. The other augurs looked up. The other augurs looked at each other. One of the other augurs asked, "Who is *that* and what is he *say*ing?"

One of the other augurs gazed up and around long enough to identify the lone speaker, then looked back, with an "Oh, just crazy old Cassandros again: says '*In the east, divine messengers*' . . . Now: —and four magpies in the south—"

"Yes, but let's have a look to the east—What?

Cass is crazy? Well, Cass may *be* crazy, as you call it, but it is after all a well-known fact that those whom the gods would inspire, they first make mad. So—"

So all the other augurs got up, though not without on the parts of some a great deal of perhaps unseemly grumbling. "You see. I could have *told* you. *Nothing* in the east. Not a single bloody bird—"

"*In the east, divine messengers!*"

The winds blew through the beard of old Cassandros, and tossed his hoary locks aloft and abroad; his staff was pointed firmly towards the quarter of the heavens called the *east*, although, of course, which was *east* or *west* or *north* or *south* depended entirely on the season of the year, the sun—unconquered as the sun doubtless is (save during eclipses: another story)—the sun rises not nor sets always throughout any year from one fixed place to another, but somewhat visibly moves its rising-place and its going-down-place as the swift seasons roll . . . Cassandros, a veteran observer of the heavens from his very earliest years, continued to point with his staff firmly towards the legal or current, east.

"He's not only mad, he's *blind*! I tell you, there's not so much as a sparrow nor a *cock*-chicken in the east!"

There was a silence; they might all, the augurs, have then sat down, and gone back to their sacred calculations: somehow, they did not. Something hung in the air, unseen. Something hung in the air, unsaid. And, so, finally, one of them said it.

"Yes . . . but . . . you know . . . not every divine messenger need *be* a *bird* . . ."

A moment more they thought on this: gainsayable it was not; then every pair of eyes turned once again. And one voice, and *not* that of Cassandros, was heard to say, "Yes . . . it *might* mean . . . lightning . . ."

To the east, they looked, and long they looked. Then one and then another said, "I see it . . .", "Yes, I see it, too . . .", "But . . . at *this* season of the year?"

And not one cried *Ibs*, nor did one, not even one, cry *Dibs*.

But one *did* say, and very gravely indeed he said it: "If that indeed is lightning, it is like no lightning I ever saw before . . ."

And, indeed, this lay beyond argument.

Some ways away, though of course still within the sacred precincts, Sir Zosimus Sulla cleared his throat. "Hem, I say, *hem*, my august and sacred brother—"

His august and sacred brother (who had been trying to recall—and to recite—a very old and very bawdy song about the allegedly bi-sexual habits of Great Caesar) said, with annoyance, "I wish to Jove you would for once and all cease interrupting me, *am* I the Brother-Superior or am I *not* the Brother-Superior . . . oh dash it all, very well, what *is* it?"

"I seem to espy a dragon in the east."

"Well, you've simply no *business* to be espying a dragon in the east; who made *you* an augur? Pay no attention, and perhaps it will go away . . . if indeed you do see one, which I doubt . . ."

"Well, you can bet your sweet senatorial buskins I *do* see one, and he's breathing flames of fire like anything."

"Oh demnition, so you do. So he is. So do I. So . . . Well, we *did* summon not merely *birds*, you know; we *did* summon '*winged creatures which fly,*' didn't we?

Slowly, *slow*ly, slowly, the two aging friends arose. And faced the east. "Yes, we *did*," said the Rev. Sir Zosimus. "We certainly *did*."

"Didn't know our own powers."

"No, we *did*n't . . . *A we*some powers, these . . ."

The silence seemed to cover not alone the entire City of New Iguvium, but the entire State of Nova Umbria; this silence was, now, first gradually, then increasingly, disturbed, and then loudly broken by the sound of the beating of great wings.

Smarasderagd came down and down and down, he circled, he rose, he descended, he went into a glide . . . a long, slow, *very* slow glide . . .

The augurs (those who had stayed put) were probably a deal more stunned than the Plebs who had stayed put (for, just as not all the augurs had believed in the hoopoe, not all the Plebs had believed in the hippo); the augurs, after all, had expected to see, in general, only what they had already seen, viz. *birds*; the others, after all, had been prepared to see, well, *any*thing . . . including, why not, a dragon . . .

"Someone's a-*ridin'* on it," said one of the Plebs.

"Them Christians can't git up nothin' like this," said another.

(Off and away, one of the Christians said to another of the Christians, "This be certainly none other than The Great Red Dragon and The Woman Clothed With the Sun—")

(Said the second Christian to the first Christian, "No, it *be*'n't. For one thing, it *be*'n't *red*—")

("What? Do you deny the evidence of things not

seen? The difference a-tween the accidents and the incidents of matter? How does you know that underneath that outer green *it be'n't really red?*")

(This was indeed a poser; still, the doubter did not immediately give up: "But *that* ain't no woman—he've got a beard on him!")

("And how does you know he be'n't a bearded woman?")

("I says that's absurd!")

("And I says, what *I* says. *I* says, I believes it a-cause it *be* absurd!")

(Such logic was remorseless as it was irresistable; they fell on their four knees, and recited, first, the Kyrie, and then the Creed, both with and without the Filioque Clause, as approved and as disapproved by the Council of Doura-Europaos which was, of course, not in Europe at all, which of course merely added to the Mystery.)

Sir Rufus, finally overcome by what he was seeing, sat down abruptly; he felt obliged to speak, but, being without words fresh and appropriate, fell back upon other, older words, to wit the Umbrian *exempla*: ". . . *panta putrespe pisipumpe*," he murmured—breaking off abruptly to snap, "Stop that silly giggling at *once*, d'you hear?"

("Cant *help* it, '*pisipumpe*'!—*al*ways used to make me giggle!")

("Chap is riding a bloody *drag*on! —I shall never allow me name to be placed with yours in the urn for lots-drawing again if I can possibly help it: *a man your age!*—Immortal gods, *rid*ing a *drag*on! —it is merely cognate with Latin *quicumque*, the *centum/pentum* change, or what do they call it; every schoolboy knows . . . A *drag*on! —*Puntes, pumperias, prusikurent, sukatu, umtu*—")

("Well, what if he *is*? Horse, hippo, dragon: with taste and scent, no argument . . . Oh I don't be*lieve* it!") ("See for yourself: *Dragon . . . Chap.*") ("Don't *mean* that . . . *'Umtu'*?") (" *'Umtu.'* ")

("Well, I shall simply throw up my hands at this, then. The syllables *umtu* have no place in any language with a claim on logical, not to say, civilized, speech . . . or do I mean, 'civilized, not to say, logical'?")

The two elders faced each other, for the moment entirely forgetful of the fact that a man riding on a dragon continued, in ever-diminishing concentric circles, to soar downwards in their direction. " *'Umtu,'* " said Sir Rufus—ignoring also the fact that much of their audience had gone rushing off from the scene of the ceremony— " 'in *umtu*, where we should expect *k* as in *fiktu*, or, in other words, Latin *ninctu*, the preservation of the labial (implied by the *m*) must result from analogy with the unsyncopated forms of the present stem, such as *umbo*, Latin *unguo*.' The book *says* so. —And besides: my throat is very sore!"

"So's mine. *Finis fandi!*" And, so saying, Sir Zosimus dipped his hands into the vessel of sacred salt and cast both handfuls into the glowing coals: it flared up beautifully.

This was to have been the signal for those summoned by Gaspar the Dreamer to rush forth and slay: slay, particularly, anybody on the list, including, *most* particularly, Peregrine . . . However. For one thing, the so-called signal, given so spontaneously by poor old Sir Zosimus, was not supposed to have been given quite yet: so, as far as *that* went, the assassins were not prepared quite yet . . .

although they had *been* prepared, of course, to slay anybody . . . anywhere . . . there are such men everywhere and everywhen. Gaspar had chosen them well, if such an ill purpose can be spoken of as *well*: but Gaspar, of course, had an excellent choice of choices: *for he knew what such men dreamed.* As he knew what such dreams were dreamed by which such men . . .

Further—

The men of sullen slumber had begun to get them up, in response to the multi-colored flickering of the salt in the fire-pits, but, though they knew this not particularly: that the salt had been cast too soon, still, something and somewhat, they knew, was not quite in order. So, though they rose, they rose not in order, nor neither in precision. And somewhat uncertain they seemed, there in the moldering Stoa, beginning to draw forth weaponry from 'neath their ragged, stained cloaks; just then—

There rushed in their direction first the one augur who had thought he had espied "an hoopoe," running willy-nilly-wildly and waving his augurial staff in order to quarter it properly; he was followed by more-or-less many of the other augurs, in hopes of doing the same (in all their minds: some future scene: "Grandfather, is it true you once espied an hoopoe?" "My child: it *is* true. *Sic* [et cætera].) —all waving *their* staffs, or, if you prefer, staves—with taste and scent, no argument—eh?—this had formed no part of any plans imprinted on the minds of these men of sullen slumber.

Further:

Peregrine's face had certainly been imprinted on their minds, not alone his naming having been inscribed upon the boards of beechwood with the baleful signs: but they had expected (without indeed having consciously so described it to themselves) to have seen the face—and figure—of Peregrine at eye-level—

Whereas *now*! *Where* was Peregrine's face? Atop, of course, Peregrine's body; but this body (mortal, as be all bodies) was now mounted atop the body of a dragon, and quite some distance above where they had expected it to be—javelins they might cast, useless though 'twere—

Meanwhile there came running towards them, by accident (but *they* knew this not) an horde of strangers waving what to some were mere staves or wands, but to others seemed as clubs—

The assassins, forgetful of, or unable to pause and to reinterpret all instructions . . . it was growing late, both late and cold . . . and seeing (and within *reach*!) wild-eyed strangers dashing down upon them (so it seemed; of course the augurs saw these strangers no more than they saw the alas non-existent *hoopoe*), at once drew their weapons.

Hard upon these augurs came, one moment afterwards, a very large part of the assembled citizenry of Nova Umbria, all in full cry, under the impression, alas equally illusory, that there was hereabouts to be seen an *hippo*: what they *did* see were strangers drawing weapons against the augurs. Uproar ceased at once; there was a horrified silence, followed by a roar of rage from the throng: to draw one's weapon against an augur was a sacrilege of the first class.

Also, a for once perfectly legitimate cause for a riot . . .

As one of the Plebs, a bath-porter by trade: *and*

a rather rough trade it was generally considered: as he now put it: "It be anyway a good arf-a-hower afore them sow-pigs and boar-pigs be praparly roasted; *SACRILEGE! SACRILEGE!*"

Barrel-staves, bung-starters, wagon-tongues, forge-hammers, wash-poles and other rude objects, were more-or-less instantly converted into weaponry; and those who had none such managed without too much difficulty to pry up the stone seats of the Stoa, the paving-blocks of such nearby squares and streets as were paved, and sundry chunks of marble from the shops of such as made grave-stones and/or graven images. The Conscript Fathers, mead dribbling down their mustard-stained mouths, moustaches, and beards, stood upon the benches and urged on the Plebs with shouts and gestures; *they* had no idea what it was all about, but they knew their duties when they saw them. (Besides, it was safer that way.)

And, overhead, each time the assassins seemed about to have the *levée-en-masse* cornered, down from the sky came Peregrine mounted upon Smarasderagd (the latter hissing and squawking in an absolute ecstacy of pleasure), and driving the would-be manslayers away from each coign (as it has been termed) of vantage.

Meanwhile, and not so very much afar off, plodded with relentless tread Baron Bruno and his five followers: of a sudden the Baron pucked up his nose and sniffed the air with hairy nostrils. "I smells 'um!" said he. Adding, "For 'e smell o' that Spynx!"

The men leered and smirked at each other at this; then they too began to sniffle and to snuffle.

One, either bolder by nature, or dazed by fatigue and so made heedless, added, "Us smells supthing else, *too*, Boss—"

"And *what*?" Sign of something, that the Baron did not, in the absence of some such phrase as, "Leave to speak, Boss?" smack the speaker with his mace.

"Dunno for sure, Boss. Supthing like a biggish snake . . . or as 't might be, a fish a-ginning to go pong . . . Boss . . ."

Further sniffs, snuffs, murmurs of assent. The Baron tested the air. The Baron growled. The Baron said nought. The six marched on. Suppose they had managed, somehow, to get up a gallop. With the foot-soldiers riding postern . . . Suppose they had gotten there so much sooner than they did. Suppose they had added their force . . . small: but drilled: disciplined . . . to the motley small swarm of madmen . . .

All history might have been different.
Not so, that it might?
Might.

The set-to in the Stoa took perhaps ten minutes.

The sudden and comparative quiet within the sacred precincts had acted much as might the removal of props from the two knight-priests. They found themselves sitting side by side, each upon a Bronze Tablet. A further sacrilege? A *nice* point. *Quis*, however, *custodiet*. And all that. No chap upon a dragon now in sight, they did not bethink them of a chap upon a dragon.

"Whom do you fancy in the first race in the Hippodrome on Opening Day?" asked Sir Zosimus.

"Fancy the Pinks," said Sir Rufus.

Sir Zosimus scoffed. "What! The *Pinks!* Why, their horses can't pull chariots for *beans*!"

"Oh what rot! —furthermore, they've got Rumbustius driving in the first race on Opening Day— look at his record—" By the universal standards of chariot-racing, those in the Hippodrome in the Capital of the Central (or Middle) Roman Empire were pretty small parsnips: but at least they were simonly and purely occasions for *chariot-racing*, and not for religious rivalry and riotry.

"Ah yes; *grant* you his *rec*ord: but whilst he was building up his *rec*ord, chap wasn't driving for the *Pinks*, he was driving for the *Puces* . . . You had better pray to Jupiter Pluvius, my advice, bunch of mudders, the Pinks' horses are: *my* advice . . . I *say*. Most everyone seems to have left the stands!"

"Shouldn't wonder; probably all gone to use the pissoir—"

"Yes yes, shouldn't wonder . . . Speaking of which . . ."

A special pair of conveniences had been rigged up for the convenience of the visiting clergy: instead of the usual second-hand pottery jars demoted for base usage when the tops had broken, these were brand-new. New or old, of course, the liquid contents were sold by Government to syndicates of tanners and fullers who used them to treat leather and wool. When a certain monarch of the old and undivided Empire had had this brilliant idea, one bold courtier dared comment, "Smelly way to make money!" —the Princely answer of course had been, *Pecunia non olet*, Money's got no smell . . . The jests of royalty tend to be both rare and very much ap-

preciated . . . particularly at the time they are uttered;
some stand the test of time much better than others.

". . . five to three, then, on the Pinks. Done?"

". . . dear chap, it would be simply taking sweet-
meats from a baby . . . Well, very well, then: *done*.!"

". . . we shall see about *that* . . . Hmm, everyone
seems to be coming back . . ."

"What? Oh. So they do. Best *we*'d be getting
back, then, too. Well, well, be over soon enough."

It had all been over in about ten minutes.

Sir Zosimus, moved by no particular rubric to
do so, but simply because he liked having once done
so, and so without much thinking, decided to do so
again—Sir Zosimus once again dipped his hands into
the vessel of sacred salt and cast both handfuls onto
the glowing coals; as before, it flamed up in a lovely
display of multi-colored flame. The returning
throng, observing the blazing colors of the salt, at
once forgot all about the bloody business it had
done, this being the way of throngs; and for that
matter, all about sundry other recently observed
events ("What silly arf-arsed hoaf claimed e'd saw a
ippo? Bloke carn't tell a ippo from a dragon . . . or
vicery-varsery! —*U*llo! *Salt*! Us must be coming in at
a good part. 'Ustle and get a proper place—")

"There: now we've all had time out to pump
bilges," said Sir Zosimus, observing the flames with
satisfaction. "What comes—"

"Forget your own *head*, next . . . 'Next' comes
me sounding the General Assembly."

"Oh yes. Quite. So it does. *Tch*."

So Sir Rufus Tiburnus proceeded to sound the

General Assembly by loudly reciting: " '*Stahitu eno deitu arsmahamo—*' "

"What-what? Not so fast. Stop a bit. 'Ar-sma*hamo*,' surely you jest?"

" 'Arsma*hamo*.' I do not jest."

"Well, if you say so," said Sir Zosimus, preparing to slip his toga over the top of his head again. If necessary.

"I *do* say so, for the *Tab*lets say so, stop in-terupting . . . Where was I? Oh. '*—arsmahamo caterahamo iouinur eno com prinuatir precarcris sacris ambretuto ape ambrefurent . . .*' Chaps don't *move.*"

"Chaps don't understand a word you're saying, precious lot *they* know about Facing fearful odds/ For the language of their fathers/ And the accents of their gods . . ."

Sir Rufus sighed a long-suffering sigh. "Hmm, of course they don't, not a word, very well then, very well." He faced the citizenry, and, his voice somewhat restored by its bit of a rest, declared right loudly, "*Men of New Iguvium and indeed of all Nova Umbria, men!*"

(The *women* were of course not present; the women, as was only seemly, were all at home, that is, gathered in one another's houses, chastely spinning and weaving: that is, actually gossiping like mad about seductions and abortions and adulteries and scandalous quarrels, the best recipes for what to do with cold roast sow; and, now and then, and in fact, very often, drawing very impolite pictures of sundry citizens (male) on the earthen floors with the tips of their distaffs, giggling rudely, nibbling barley-and-cheese and eggs and filberts and apples, rubbing out the drawings with many a scornful snort; in general having the time of their lives and, incidentally, avoiding all the cold drafts whistling about the sacred precincts.)

"*Men of New Iguvium and indeed of all Nova Umbria*," barked Sir Rufus, through cupped hands, " '*Arrange yourselves in priestly and in military ranks, Men of Iguvium!*' "

The women, who could hear him quite clearly . . . who was it said that no city should be so large that the voice of a single herald could not be heard throughout it? . . . doesn't matter . . . New Iguvium qualified . . . the *Women* of New Iguvium, who could hear him quite clearly, imitated his citified accents, and laughed like anything. The *Men* of New Iguvium, well, the arrangement was done, though not without a great deal of unseemly shuffling. It had, after all, not been done in some while, and some of the younger men of either category proved reluctant to accept the directions of older ones who claimed to remember the proper arrangements (and didn't), but it was at length *done*.

The two knightly priests now passed along the ranks, Sir Zosimus Sulla trotting as rapidly as was consistent with dignity, only pausing now and then to say to perfect strangers, "Good to see you again," "Knew your father," "At school with your uncle, delightful chap," and "Much good hunting lately?"—

—whereas Sir Rufus Tiburnus, who had thrice commanded legions (once against the Paphlagonians and twice against the Borborygmians), moved along more slowly, with now and again such comments as, "Shoe-latchets don't match, take that man's name," "Call this a purple stripe on your *toga virilis*, Boy?

Shamed of yourself!'' and ''Ah. Padre Sahib: all
seems in order. Credit to your caste . . .''

Meanwhile: Peregrine. Who said now, to
Smarasderagd, ''Well, I really must thank you for
this ride. And now, I think . . .''

Really, he had only just begun to move away
and had not really moved more than an inch or two;
Smarasderagd snagged him neatly by slipping one
talon in between Peregrine's toe and sandal-thong.
''Not to be in such a hurry,'' said the dragon. ''I am
really fearfully hungry; all that flying upwind really
takes it out of one.''

''I am sure that I smell roast pork, and—''

The reptile flicked his nictitating membranes at
him. '' 'Roast pork!' *What?* Do you think I am car-
nivorous? If I were, I'd have eaten *you*, long ago!''

Peregrine, considering this, shuddered, even
though just a little bit. ''The wind, you know,'' he
said. ''Hungry are you? *Well . . .*''

Sir Zosimus, as Junior Brother, now declared
the Ritual Edict of Banishment on Enemy Aliens,
Followers of Infamous Professions, Vagrants,
Mashers and Loiterers: as this was a common, as well
as secular, declaration, everyone else had heard it
heaps of times; and some of the less patriotic in fact
flagrantly picked their noses during its recital. But
even these, however, listened with great interest to
the next item: namely, the Ritual Curse Against All
Enemies Far and Near, to wit: '' 'On that tribe and
that tribe and the other tribe and any other tribe
within the meaning of the Criminal Tribes Acts, and
on that village and that village and the other village
and on any other village within the meaning of the

Contumacious Villages Act, and on the chief citizens in office and the chief citizens not in office, upon the young men in arms and upon the young men not in arms, enemies of this name and that name and any other name: *Anhostatu tursitu tremitu hondu holta ninctu nepitu sonita sauita preplotatu preuilatu* . . . .

" 'Terrify them and cause them to tremble and cast them down into the depths of Hell, overwhelm them with snow and douse them with water, deafen them with thunder and blind them with lightning, and wound and mutilate and trample them down and beat them up and bind them hand and foot!' "

This went over *very* well. From all sides were heard growls of, "Ah, that's the stuff: teach *them* to go a-stealin of our goats and pigs—" "Aye, an' lettin they chickings inter our spelt-fieldses!" "Us 'asn't 'eard such a good old-fashioned solid all-round curse in *years:* what be next?"

Next, three more hogs were sacrficed (boars, this time), and the Benediction was invoked: as follows, " 'We invoke the immortal gods to grant to the City of New Iguvium and the State of Nova Umbria, to the men and women and children, to the beasts and fruits and fields thereof, success in word and deed, before and behind, in private and in public, in vow and augury and sacrifice. Be favorable and propitious with thy peace, and keep the Iguvians and the Umbrians safe. Keep safe the magistrates, the priesthoods, the Plebs, and the lives of all men and women and children, of fields and fruits and beasts and bees and hives. O thou and those who be invoked, we invoke thee. In truth we invoke thee.' "

On reaching the conclusion of these few words of simple piety, Sir Zosimus paused. "I say, that's rather touching. Felt *touched*."

"Felt so meself," Sir Rufus concurred. "Felt distinctly touched."

"Signal to me secretary to jot 'em down in his tabulae directly, is what I shall do."

The signal was indeed given: the recipient, however, was not Sir Zosimus's secretary (a learned Greek from Philadelphia Antigonia, who had gone to answer that call which e'en king and queen must answer here below), but—the good knight's eyesight no longer being of the keenest—the recipient was an immensely worn and blackened image of exceedingly inferior marble, believed by the Old Pagans to be that of Pismo Krapuvius (Crapovious) (Grabovius), an extremely minor deity of whom absolutely nothing else was known; boys too young to have to pay the two groats admission-fee to The Bath were, merely upon uttering the syllables, *Pismo Krapuvius*, allowed in for free—whereas the *Neo*-Pagans, who were as down on worshipping idols as any Christian, maintained it was a simulacrum of the notorious Empress Messalina, stripped for her own bath, and/or, conceivably, any other purpose or purposes, but be all this as it may . . .

The Quæstor, misinterpreting both pause and signal, approached (though not too closely) and announced, "Your Holinesses will now proceed to chase the chosen sacred heifers."

"—chase the *what*?—"

". . . heifers . . ."

"Me dear chap, *we* are not going to chase any heifers, sacred or profane. What do you take us for and how young do you think we *are*?"

The Quæstor, whose place had for so long been

a mere sinecure, wiped his face upon his sacred mantle, and said, with a slight sigh, "Ah, but Your Holinesses would naturally not be expected to chase them in propriae personae, but by proxy."

"Our Holinesses *would*n't?"—Sir Zosimus.

"Ah well that's an ox of a different color." —Sir Rufus. "Long as it's by proxy, chase what you like: heifers, girls, boys, nanny-goats, cameleopards . . ."

The sacred heifers, lowing lugubriously, were chased by proxy, that is, several yokels who had previously hobbled them, now proceeded to round them up, after which they were officially surreptitiously exchanged for an equal number of swine; the local taste holding that eating heifer was like chewing *gum*, i.e., the oozy resin of the mastic tree, which grew thereabouts as common as filberts.

Sir Zosimus now suddenly produced a sound like a whinny; Sir Rufus said he begged his pardon, Sir Zosimus repeated it more slowly.

" '*Eehiianasum.*' "

"*Oh*. To be sure. '*Eehiianasum,*' that's Oscan, isn't it?"

"*Course* it's Oscan. Means 'chasing the sacred heifers.' "

"Oh. To be sure . . . Succinct sort of language, one might call it."

"Onomatopœia, one might call it, too."

Sir Zosimus looked at him gravely. "*Shouldn't*, though. Natives might not understand."

And, at just that moment, there was a distinct sort of *Sound* . . . to be precise, *two* distinct sorts of Sounds: the first being quite indescribable; the second very easily describable: this being caused by

everyone present attempting at once to go somewhere
else with the utmost speed . . . and deciding, very
suddenly, not to go so after all. There *is*, after all,
very little point in trying to walk or even run away
from a dragon . . . even a dragon coming along on
foot . . .

Smarasderagd came waddling and walking and
wiggling and slithering along. He might have, had he
cared to have, left destruction in his wake. He did not
care to, and, in fact, did his best to go round rather
than over . . . or through . . . whatever stood in his
way . . . This was of course not always possible: for
example, a batch of wet cement . . . Even several centuries later the local residents were pointing out to
visitors, "And there be the *foot*prints of the dragon
. . . And *that* be its *tail* . . ."

Smarasderagd came round about the spinial and
did his best not to knock over any of the rather tot-
tery walls, gates, and what-have-you. He came, as we
say, along . . . and he was, as we have seen (and even
if we haven't) a rather *long* dragon. And he came up
to within a certain distance of the two visiting priests
(six cubits and a span, as some would have it; others
would not have it at all). He stopped. He asked,
"*You called?*"

There was a certain silence.

Sir Zosimus to Sir Rufus: "*You* are the Brother-
Superior. *Answer it!*"

Sir Rufus: "Hem. Ah. Well. Hum. Mmm . . .
We *did?*"

Smarasderagd: "You certainly *did*. 'Wingèd
creatures which fly.' *Did*n't you?"

"Er, *hemph* . . . Well, put like *that*, well, *yes*. I
suppose we *did*."

Sir Zosimus: "*A*wfully nice of you to come."

There was a pause.

Then, "You must be rather tired, after your journey."

"I am *very* tired after my journey."

"Perhaps you'd like to wash up, then?"

"I have already washed up. In the piscina."

Another pause. The fact is, that however well-educated a man may be, be he patrician, knight, priest, or what*ev*er he may be, small talk with dragons is not usually among his abilities. It may be because of this, that, by and by and in after years, every court and castle contained on its payroll someone whose particular duty was to *slay* dragons, how disgusting, but with the decay of empire the arts of conversation and the tolerance for the odd and the curious suffered severe declines; one could hardly imagine, say, Pliny the Elder, feeling obliged to send someone out to slay a dragon; he would have talked the poor creature to death instead, probably.

"Well, ah, mmm . . . I say! You'd probably like something to *eat*, *would*n't you?"

"Yes yes! The roast sow is all ready, and the roast boar—"

Smarasderagd showed his teeth. Even Sir Rufus, who had been three times in charge of legions and had, purely for sport, once chased griffins in Arimaspia, took a step backward. "*Flesh?*" asked Smarasderagd. "I *never* eat flesh. It gives me a heartburn upon—well, never mind that. It is however very nice of you to have asked. And, as I was sure that you would, I have already dined. I have eaten the fish in the piscina."

This prompted from, of all people, the Quæstor,

the rather startled question of, "What? *All* of them?"

Smarasderagd turned his head rather slowly, identified the source of the question—a question which he seemed to regard as in no way unreasonable—and said, "Oh no. Not all of them. Merely the carp, the turbot, the lampreys, the mullet, and the eels. The trash-fish (and, of course, all minnows, fingerlings, and fry) I have as a matter of principle left . . . for *you* . . ." It was perhaps not entirely clear, Smarasderagd having moved his head somewhat, if the *you* were singular or plural. No one, however, cared to ask. The question of the fish in the piscina was, as a matter of fact, and as we are on the subject, a rather interesting one. For ages immemorial, they had been known as "the sacred fish in the Piscina." It was long the custom to go and feed them, as symbols of fertility, or whatever, particlarly on holy days and festivals. The first influx of Christians might, one would think, have tempted some of these zealous saints to have done the sacred fish some mischief: not so. It had after all, had it not, been discovered in the Christian Sibylline Books that the initial letters (in the Greek alphabet) of

Ἰησους
Χρειστὸς
Θεοῦ
Ὑιὸς
Σωτὴρ

(*Jesus Chreistos Theou Uios Soter*, Jesus Christ Son of God Savior), spelled ΙΧΘΥΣ or *Ichthys*, which means, of course, *fish* . . . ? It had. Pretty soon every dusty place throughout the Roman Empire was filled

with people scratching very impressionistic outlines
of *fish* in the dust . . . sometimes with their sticks,
sometimes with their fingers, even in some cases with
their toes . . . and next rolling their eyes around to see
who would come sidling up to them with an offer to
act as guides to the nearest catacombs: also, for
reasons obscure to the local yokels of New Iguvium,
those of the Newer Persuasion had a devotion for
*eat*ing fish . . . on a certain day of the week . . . *could*
such be termed as *meats offered to idols*? —evidently
they could not. The trade was clandestine (on behalf
of both religions), but the trade was brisk.

And if the Quæstor now received the news that
the biggest and best of these fish had been all in one
meal consumed by a dragon—if the Quæstor seemed
somewhat less than immensely pleased, can this be
taken as evidence for the sempiternal rumors that the
Quæstor connived at the sales of the sacred fish . . .
for a share of the profits?—Which of us, indeed, can
say?

The Quæstor, at least, for the immediate
moment, was saying nothing more at all.

Sirs Rufus Tiburnus and Zosimus Sulla for a
moment more stood in a bemused manner, mur-
muring (once again) to each other, "Awesome
powers, these . . . *A we*some powers . . ."

Then, Sir Rufus recollecting himself, his position, and what he owed to it, suddenly snapped—if
not precisely to Attention, to something rather close
to it—and, with a bow somewhat between medium
and deep, said, "Well. Jolly decent of you to come.
And, ah, now that you are, ah, *here* . . . is there
anything in particular which we can do to make your
stay a pleasant one?"

Smarasderagd did not give this polite enquiry

very long consideration. "No, no," he said. "No, nothing, I think, in particular. I was summoned. I came. I am now, or soon will be, I take it, free to depart—"

"Yes yes! Oh certainly!"

"Free? By all means. Feel free, quite free to—"

The dragon, however, was not yet finished. "—and so, inasmuch as I *have* come all this very long way in response to your summons, I propose to withdraw myself to the farther end of these precincts in order to take some repose without . . . I trust . . . in the least inconveniencing you . . . and in the meanwhile I shall observe the rest of the ceremonies with interest. With deep interest. *If I may.*"

They assured him, all of them, that he indeed might: though of course they tried not to sound excessively, and certainly not impolitely, eager.

It was more or less precisely at this point that a strange voice was heard . . . strange, at any rate, to the Rev. Sir Rufus Tiburnus, Pat., Kt., SPQR Proconsul (Ret.), and to the Rev. Sir Zosimus Sulla, Pat., Kt. Senatusconsultum de Bachanalibus (Ret.) . . . heard saying, "Can I get off now, Smarry? 'Your Dragonic Greatness,' I mean? Can I, now? Hey?"

And Peregrine's head, which had, as had the rest of him, been hidden from sight by several of the dragon's coils as well as both of the dragon's wings, was now seen peeping out: and with a most pleading expression on his face. Sir Rufus gave a start. Sir Zosimus made a little jump, or perhaps it was a very small hop. The Quæstor did nothing at all. And from the seats round about the single side of the sacred precincts where the seats had not fallen in, came the sound of voices saying such things as, "Ahr, *that* be

the chap as come a-ridin' in on the dragon!'', "What
do it *mean*, does yer suppose?'', "Blessed if h*I* know:
something *big*, what h*I* suppose!'' and so forth. And
so on.

"Chap who was riding the dragon,'' said Sir
Rufus.

"Very same chap, indeed,'' said Sir Zosimus.

"Want to get off now?'' asked Smarasderagd.
"*All* right, then. Shan't need you anymore, anyway.
—Hop it, then!''

Peregrine hopped. He had begun to stamp his
feet to get the cramps out when he suddenly seemed
to notice whom he was facing.

"Very respectful and reverent greetings to Your
Very Reverend Sirs,'' he said. (Smarasderagd was by
then proceeding to waddle, wiggle, slither, and otherwise make his long way down the long ruinous
reaches of the sacred precincts.)

"Chap seems nicely spoken,'' said Sir Rufus.

"Yes, yes. Evidently gently bred. —Little bit
more than a *lad*, though. Brave enough to ride a
dragon, though. —I say, Rufe, doesn't he seem, hm,
doesn't he seem a bit familiar about the form and
face?''

Sir Rufus gave Perry a long, reflective look. "By
Jove. See what you mean. *Does* look familiar. Hm.
Hm. *Ha!* Tell you what: he looks like that lad we
were at school with, rustic lad, still, he could construe very well, you know, Zos: construe better than
you. What *was* the boy's name? Called him '*Pal*,'
what we called him.''

Memory thus nudged, Sir Zosimus cried, "Yes
we did! He was an official hostage, I seem to recall,
came from Sipodalla, or some such—''

But Pergerine's memory was also being nudged;

"Oh, you're *right!*" he exclaimed. "My father *was* a hostage! *His* father, old King Cumnodorius, was getting ready to sign a peace treaty with a Caesar and so Dada had to go down and get to be a hostage while they were ironing out the details and they made him go to school . . . Yes! He *told* me!" He beamed at the two old men and the two old men beamed at him; he suddenly remembered to say, "And the name of our country is, you really must excuse me, *Sapodilla*, and my father's name is Paladrine and his family name is Pal—"

"Yes yes! You've got his very voice, me boy; his very voice! Except your accent's a bit better, don't mind me saying so; yes: his family name was Palæo-something-or-other. '*Pal*,' what we called him."

"*Pal* . . . Yes yes . . ."

There was a lot more beaming. Sir Zosimus said, "*Well*, Prince—"

Perry was perforce obliged to interrupt. "No, sirs, *not* 'Prince.' My father the King has three legitimate sons, but I am not one of them; and that in fact is why . . . indirectly, of course . . . is why I am here: the ancient laws of Sapodilla require that all the king's bastard sons be banished on their eighteenth birthdays, to make sure we don't try to seize the throne, you see; under penalty of 'never returning either alone or with armed host, on penalty of being flayed alive in order to maintain the Peace of the Realm'—nothing personal about any of it, of course: it's the *law*."

Sir Rufus said, "Yes, yes, quite see that, makes sense of a sort. Now what *I* used to do with *my* bastards, made 'em all bankers, is what *I* did; what used you to do with your bastards, Zos?"

"Made 'em publishers," said Sir Zosimus.

"*Some*body's got to do it . . . Well, well, politics: *one* thing. Welcoming the son of an old school chum, begat *this* side of the blanket or other side of the blanket: another. Allow me to embrace you, me boy."

Sir Rufus claimed the same privilege, then they all beamed at each other once again, and then they began to discuss such matters as King Paladrine's health and related matters ("Still so fond of palindromes, is he? He *is*? He *is*!"), when a quite new sound was brought to all their ears.

And a quite new sight.

"You *see*," Sir Zosimus said, in a quite low voice to Sir Rufus. "What did I tell you? *Barbarian incursions!*"

And right down what had once been the Imperial Way came the *tramp-tramp-tramp* of heavily-armed men, three of them on foot and three of them on horseback.

And in the lead was Baron Bruno.

He saw Peregrine, if not the first thing he saw, as the first-most thing in the way of immediate business. And at him he pointed his mailed fist.

"*You!*" he growled. "A precious chase yer've led me, and hI means ter make yer pay fer it. Bind jer in chains, h'is the least of what hI means . . ."

Perry recognized at any rate both the Baron's manner and the Baron's banner, and, also, that whatever other success his trick had had, back at Alf High Town, it had not prevented the High King's brutal brother-in-law from tracking him *here* . . . *here* . . . *all the way here* . . . and with a very great deal of very evident malice aforethought . . . afterthought . . . and, most importantly, present-thought . . . .

Sir Rufus Tiburnus wasted not a moment on low-voiced comments. In the same way in which he had already once that day sounded the General Assembly, he now did so again: this time, however, he skipped the original Umbrian. His voice may have been slightly hoarse, but it was very clear and very calm. "Men of New Iguvium and of all Nova Umbria," he began his orders, "Form in military and in priestly ranks." The men of New Iguvium and of all Nova Umbria had already had this command once today and so by this its second time they were much quicker about it. For all that they knew to the contrary, the three men on horse and the three men on foot were but the first of hordes; if so . . . well, time enough to see what "if so" . . . in the meanwhile, they recognized that they were under not only Imperial orders, but under experienced Imperial orders. They formed.

The Baron drew his own men to a halt. His eyes flickered rapidly from side to side. He considered.

Now the men of the priestly ranks, during the day's first General Assembly, realizing that the occasion was purely and entirely *pro forma*, had then said nothing. *Now*, they realized, was different. *Quite* different. Their main duty had always been (long though since they had had the chance of publicly performing it) to utter imprecations against enemy invaders. And they now began to utter them. These were not at once clearly heard; for one, their lips at first moved silently; for another, Sir Rufus Tiburnus was giving *his* orders—

"*By the right flank—!*"

Then the voices of the priestly ranks rose next

to a whisper and then to a murmur and thence to a mutter and thence to an absolutely blood-crawling weirdly wailing ancient-of-days and throat-tighteningly threatening . . .

"Right-*wheel*! Swords *out!*"

". . . *tetter and tettany . . . ball-crawl, night-crawl and nightmare . . .*" they ululated. Baron Bruno's troops began to show the first signs of uneasiness. Their eyes shifted, their eyes rolled. ". . . *wang-warts, weewee weevils, hamstringing and her-nia . . .*"

"Left-*flank*! Column of *threes!*"

". . . *crotch-rot and crapulence and issues of the flesh, and eye-dribble and ear-wiggle . . .*

"Close up those *ranks*, Men of Iguvium! *One-*two-three-four—"

". . . *suppurations of the groins . . . in-continence of urine, of fœces, and of sperm . . .*"

The troops of the Baron Bruno, who knew but very well that they were *not* but the first of hordes and that absolutely nothing lay behind them, save the long, long way they had come, began to grow extremely uneasy. The Baron, if had begun to do anything of the sort, did not show it; he merely growled, "Do as h*I* does." It was his intention to withdraw towards one of the more ruined sides—towards the very end, in fact—of the sacred precincts, and there—

But as for *there*, where there was, as the keen eyes of Baron Bruno had clearly seen, nought but a grass-covered series of hillocks: suddenly there was nothing of the sort *there*: there *was* indeed a "there" there, and this *there* now, not suddenly, but rather very quickly gradually, was revealed to be the form

of a dragon . . . not perhaps one of your very largest
dragons, but perhaps (per*haps*?) one large enough to
do for six men, only three of whom were mounted
and all of whom were tired. Smarasderagd did not
leap, he merely rose up . . . and straightened himself
out . . . and out . . . and out . . . and then he gave a
hiss like one of those engines which, employing
steam, perform such amusing tricks in some of the
larger metropolises: Alexandria, for example: and
then he issued forth a few of his medium-longer-sized
flames of fire . . . and a mini-mesial squawk—

"In close *ranks*," directed Sir Rufus, exactly as
though he had the full force of the Borborygmians
(or, for that matter, the Paphlagonians) to deal with.
"*For-ward*, MARCH!"

Baron Bruno was no coward. But he was no
fool, either. He held up his mailed fist. This might
have been a defiance. This might have been a sub-
mission. This might have been a salute.

He wheeled slowly, ponderously, around on his
weary horse. He needed give no new command.
Then, followed by his five weary men, he departed as
he had come.

And one swift, sullen glance he cast at Peregrine
as he passed.

"Demned impudence of the fellow," growled
Sir Rufus, the scouts having assured him that the
small army was indeed gone away . . . going slowly,
to be sure, for it was, to be sure, a tired small army
. . . very small . . . very tired . . . but going the way it
had come: to wit: *away*. "Demned impudence of the
fellows, trying to try on their Barbarian, or, if you
like, for I like to be fair, their semi-Barbarian incur-

sions, when there haven't even been any proclaimed
for this year yet. Well, let him pass the word along:
we are ready."

Sir Zosimus had his own comment. "What
comes next?" he asked.

Informed that they had just won a glorious vic-
tory and that their lands and houses and indeed their
everything else was not going to be pillaged and
destroyed; and that the sacrificial meats were now
ready for distribution, the citizenry gave three cheers,
and again three cheers, and next came, if not running, then anyway walking very, very fast, although
in strict order of precedence, to receive their portions
of the roasted swine: those who had dishes, upon
dishes; those who had no dishes, upon trenchers;
those who had no trenchers, upon the points of their
knives: and those who lacked by reason of poverty,
even knives, simply and modestly (or immodestly)
lifted up a corner of a garment to which the addition
of any amount of grease could make no difference
whatsoever. And those who got no crackling were
allowed an extra piece of piglet instead, and a chunk
of chitterlings apiece.

Some of the Paganry were, it is to be feared, alas
intolerant enough to shove portions of these savory
roasts under the noses of such Christians as chanced
to be encountered round about, and to taunt them
with such cries as, "Don't *that* smell *good*?" and,
"Wouldn't *you* like to have some?" The Christians
were perforce bound to shudder, and, with murmurs
of, " '. . . *blood, things strangled, and meats offered
to idols*,' feh! and fui!," to turn righteously away:
but now and then their nostrils were observed to
quiver.

(Some of some of the yokels next looked round
to see if they could see any Jews, and try the same
taunt; none, however, were to be seen. Reuben, in
fact, was at that very moment at home discussing
with Simeon the hypothetical case of a man, who
having been directed to give his wife a bill of
divorcement, chooses to write it, instead of on, say,
papyrus or parchment, some other substance;
"Valid," said Simeon. "Even upon, say . . . horn?"
asked Reuben. "Valid," said Simeon. "And suppose
he writes it on the horn of a cow? Still valid?" "Only
if she gets to keep the cow," said Simeon. "Say,
there's been a lot of noise outside, hasn't there?" he
asked—somewhat rhetorically, one might think.
"Wonder what it is?" "Go know," said Reuben.
"—And sup*pose* . . .")

Meanwhile, back at the sacred precincts, the Official Perquisites for the visiting College of Priests
were being brought out and counted out upon a large
table with a raised rim. The secretary of Sir Rufus
was weighing and enumerating them. "One bushel of
golden emmerods," he announced.

The secretary of Sir Zosimus said, "*Check.*"

"*Item*, one peck of gold mice."

"*Check.*"

"*Item*, three gold rings for the Elder Brother
and three gold rings for the Younger Brother."

"*Check.*"

"*Item*, one silver tassy for the Elder Brother and
one silver tassy for the Younger Brother."

"*Check.*"

There they all were, and everyone was allowed to
file past and have a good gander at them all. "*Well,*"
said Sir Rufus, "been a tiring trip and a tiring day,
so—"

Peregrine said, "Sir—"

"Not without its interest, its exitement, and its satisfactions, though," commented Sir Zosimus.

"Sir—"

"—so I suggest that we all retire and have a good old lie-down. Then I suggest we all go for a nice dip in The Baths—baths still working, here?"

"*Sir!*"

"Ah. 'Heated them up especially for the occasion,' eh? *Very* well!"

"*Oh*, SIR!"

The two knights faced him with some small measure of surprise and displeasure. "Now, young man—" "Now, boy—" "What is it, d'you want to come along? *Cer*tainly you may come along, but—" "Not the thing, you know, these iterations and interruptions. Sure your father would be the first to agree, so—"

"Oh, but, Sir: *Look!*"

They did look: and just in time to see Smarasderagd, without a single previously audible sound, and unnoticed by anyone save Peregrine, come gliding and swooping down and clutch hold of the entire table with all its gorgeous contents, and go swooping off aloft again, *this* time beating his immense wings and issuing triumphant *squawks*, amidst which and despite the shouts of the knights, might be identified such phrases as, ". . . revolution . . . oppression . . . reparation . . . exploitation . . ." and "*trash-fish* . . ."

The knights shouted, showed their fists, drew their swords, called upon the archers (there were no archers), and then, as the dragon and all his gains vanished off into the most remote distance, fell silent . . . Only, rather a bit off, the augur Cassandros muttered, "*In the east, Divine Messengers . . .*"; but Cassandros himself was, of course, rather a bit off.

Sir Zosimus, as one has perhaps by now observed, tended to be a bit repetitious. "What comes next?" he enquired.

The Quæstor it was, this time, who replied. "What comes next, Your Holinesses," he said, "is that we disburse to Your Holinesses the Official Perquisites, to wit and videlicet, one bushel of golden emmerods; *Item*, one peck of—"

Sir Rufus was furious. "Why, what do you mean, you demned old Quæstor, isn't that what you've already done? And see—just see—with what result—!"

"Oh, *no*, Your Holinesses," said the Quæstor, softly. "Not at all. What we have already shown were merely simulacra. Made of brass for the most part, and of, merely, silver wash, for another."

Sir Rufus was *still* furious. "*What?* D'you mean you intended to *cheat* us?"

Still softly, said the Quæstor, "Oh, *no*, Your Holinesses. Oh not at *all*. It is merely that experience has shown us, here in New Iguvium and indeed in all Nova Umbria, that sometimes the sight of treasures acts as a temptation, and therefore as a cause of theft. So we *always* show the fakes first . . . although I admit that we have never had a *dragon* to contend with before: still, it shows the wisdom of our ancestors, as wise today as the day that it were uttered. —Treasure-bearers! Bring forth the genuine treasures!"

Gradually, as, item by item by item, the *real* Official Perquisites were produced and displayed once again, the faces of the elder knights and priests resettled into peaceful lines. Then Sir Rufus fired up all over again. "Why, you demned fool of my secretary, what do you mean by weighing out *brass* as though it were *gold*? I've more than half a mind to feed you to me lampreys back home!"

And, yet again, yet again, the Quæstor had the final word. "Oh, Your Holinesses, it was not the fault of your secretary. *We had switched the scales* . . ."

Sir Rufus's face was a study in mixed emotions; on the one hand, he felt that, regardless of this and of that, it was no way to treat an Imperial official . . . and, on the other hand, as in a moment recollected, it was, really, more or the less the same way that had been used at the Comitium, where, with dishonest ballots and of course purely for the good of the Imperium, he and his colleague had been elected (or, perhaps, at any rate, selected) for the sacred Imperial offices which they still held.

So, in a moment, he cleared his throat, and said, "Very much obliged to you, I'm sure."

The Quæstor bowed deeply. At this moment, up came the secretary of Sir Zosimus Sulla, Pat. (*Need we go through all these titles yet again? Did Livy? Did Plutarch? Did Isidore of Seville?*), and, saying, "Your Excellency will recollect having asked me to remind you of this," bowed, and withdrew. The *this* was a rather long cylinder of pressed leather, and affixed to it were three immense wax seals, two medium-sized lead seals, one somewhat smaller silver seal . . . and one very, *very* small gold seal. Sir Zosimus gazed at it. "Quite forgot," said he. After a second's thought, he laboriously opened it. Out rolled a parchment of familiar size and shape and decoration, even if its contents were not at once obvious. Sir Zosimus began to real aloud—having, in a

stage aside, reminded those near to hand that it had
been "handed to me just as we were setting out
hither; 'sailing under sealed orders,' as you might
say; not to be opened until . . . until . . . well well:
*op*ened, i'n't it: so let's get on . . ."

It began, as documents of the sort invariably
did, I THE AUGUST CAESAR, continued with
Princeps Dux Imperatorque, and, within the com-
pass of a remarkably few lines, managed to include
not only every land over which every or rather any
Roman emperor anywhere had ever reigned but every
single tribe or nation, clan, horde, mob, group or
even clump of Barbarians over which and with any
Roman emperor had ever claimed a conquest, treaty,
or confœderation . . .

 . . . *seeing that it has pleased the immortal gods
to summon* . . .

 . . . *wherefore* . . .

 . . . *inasmuchas* . . .

 . . . *nor may the curial nor the magistral chairs
vacant be* . . .

 . . . *therefore reposing* . . .

Sir Zosimus read it all, he read every bit of it all;
after all, it was for the greater part in Latin and the
rest in Greek: and contained not a single syllable of
Umbrian: so it was no great task *to* read it all . . .
There was a silence, following the inevitable *and may
the immortal gods save the Senate and the People of
Rome* . . . Then Sir Zosimus asked, "*Who* in Jove's
name is *G. Zumzumius Aquifer*?"

"Precisely *my* question," said Sir Rufus.

Once again it fell to the Quæstor to reply; at one
time his office had been more-or-less confined to that
of public treasurer, but . . . and, at any rate, once the
ceremonial part of the services were over he had been

feeling a great deal more at ease with these importunate (though of course exceedingly honorable) foreign—in a manner of speaking—dignitaries . . . once again it fell to the Quæstor to speak in answer to the question.

"Cnaeus Zumzumius Aquifer, Your Holinesses," he said, "was Sub-Imperial-sub-Legate here to Himself The August Caesar, until it pleased the immortal gods to remove him from all duties here below, of a cachexy of the bowels, whilst at stool, the third day after the Gules of August, *ult*."

A pause. "Chap's *dead*," then observed Sir Zosimus.

"Your Holinesses. Quite."

And Sir Rufus said, "We seem to be charged with appointing his successor, while we're here."

"Your Holinesses. Quite."

A longer pause. Then, "Pray don't look at *me*," said Sir Zosimus. "Wouldn't touch it with a ten-foot pole; climate would kill me off in a month."

His Elder Brother cleared his elder throat. "Much as I of course feel and believe that a public office is a public trust," said he, "still . . . me family . . . me age . . . me infirmities . . ."

They looked at each other. Then they looked at their chief-most local informant. And with one voice said, "Quæs*tor!*"

The Quæstor drew himself up. The Quæstor looked all about him with an air of infinite triumph. The Quæstor's eye met one local eye. Then another. And another. And . . . "I greatly fear, and alas, Your Holinesses," the Quæstor said, "that it really would not do . . ."

And, after a moment's reflection, the two visiting knights conceded that, really, it would *not* do. "Local chap. Factionalism. Feuds. Gensual ties. Obligations.—No No. Wouldn't *do*," they agreed. They stood in thought, in the rapidly cooling air. No one said anything. No one, that is, said a word. Peregrine, however, did make a sound. He had *had* a *very* long ride on the dragon; then he'd been standing in the open precincts for quite some time sneaking here a glance and there a glance and considering his chances of a tactful, if brief, sneak-off . . . Peregrine broke wind.

"A sign!" cried . . . someone. And someone else, "*A sign!*"

And, such being the extraordinary popular delusion and the madness of crowds: "*A sign!*" cried everybody else. "*A sign! A sign!*"

Before Peregrine knew what was up (or even down) he was on his knees, the knights were tapping his shoulders with their swords and thrusting their rings at him to kiss, and all around him were such phrases being rattled off as:

". . . Peregrine the son of Paladrine . . ."

". . . the grandson of Cumnodorius Rex Confœderatatus to and of . . ."

". . . the Divine Guphus, sometime Himself the August Caesar Princeps Dux Imperatorque . . ."

". . . and now deified . . ."

". . . if illegitimate, we legitimate thee . . ."

". . . in unnaturalized, we naturalize thee . . ."

". . . if unqualified, we qualify thee . . ."

And, there coming finally a pause, as finally there must, Sir Zosimus came to the rescue with one of his last unrecited Umbrian paradigms, or whatever, and, in a tone immensely hieratic and impressive, intoned: "*Slagim, pusme, snata* . . ." and added, by his tone, in evident conclusion: "*Ars-*

mahamo, arsmahamo, arsmahamo.'' Turning to the
throng, for the most part gnawing the last bits of
gristle off the sacrifical swine bones, and burping
with contentment and loyalty, he announced, ''Men
of New Iguvium and indeed of all Nova Umbria, I
now present to you your new Sub-Imperial-sub-
Legate, P. Peregrine Paleosomethingorother. Obey
him in all things, d'you hear, you clods? And he's to
collect all the imposts the Quæstor doesn't snaffle
first and to keep what he likes in return for defending
and ruling you, save only he's supposed to send on to
the Capitol one-half of one-half a half, plus one-
quarter of one-quarter plus one-half-a-quarter, to
pay the Legions, you oafs, d'you hear? And if *not*,
then the Burgundians and the Borborygmians and
the Boogeymenses will all come down and bite your
bottoms raw, and so save you right: and now let's
hear three *Ave*s and a tiger!''

They heard it.

But whilst all *this* was going on, the augurs had
not ceased to try to tally up their totals in order to
produce a single sensible augury to bring the day to
an official conclusion: otherwise, what right had they
to their titles?—None. ''Three starlings . . . No, I tell
you it was six starlings . . . and then the woodpeckers
. . . No *NO* the hoopoe does *NOT* count . . . crows
. . .'' and, ''Yes yes of course we've done the dragon,
old Cassandros and his—''

And then, and then alone, old Cassandros
slowly turned from his look of long fetch, and, his
whited locks all a-blowing and his beard looking like
card-wool in a gale, asked:

''Did no one accompt the ibis in the east?''

''*What* 'ibis in the east'? I swan, Cass, if you
aren't—''

"I preach the bird as I see it," said old Cassandros. And no more.

This previously unprojected prognostication throwing all previous reckonings completely off and out, the augurs perforce had to reckon all over again. And, at last, to conclude, that, although twas indeed very odd: all the same, twas very clear; *or*, as some would have it, although twas very clear, still, twas very odd . . .

The cheers for selection of the newest official had just died down when the augurs in a body approached the visiting priests. "Ah yes. Augur chaps. *Birds.* 'Cheep-cheep,' what? Haw haw. Just our little jest. And what is Your Birdyships's official prognostication?"

The Chief Augur pointed to the exceedingly worn old Obelisk, and/or Simulacrum . . . Pismo Krapuvius? Messalina? Castor without Pollux? Who the hell *knows*?

"You see, Your Holinesses, the Lines of Descansion run right along through *here*. And the Haruspexual Lines run right along through *there*. And where they intersect, as any f—*hem*-a-hem—as anyone may plainly see, is *here*. By yon time-blackened piece of masonry, or stone, termed the Obelisk . . . or Simulacrum . . ."

"Yes yes."

"Yes yes."

". . . and the meaning of the auspices is that an incription must be inscribed upon the said stone according to immemorial custom—"

"Oh, get on with it, get *on* with it: *What* is the inscription?"

The Chief Augur, and indeed, all the other augurs, looked at Sir Rufus (who had interrupted)

with a, and in fact with more than a, touch of
reproof.

"It is a very awesome inscription, Sacred Sires:
and this is how it goes: *If two black oxen make doodoo here* . . ."

It was, all agreed (the Jews did not count;
neither did the Christians: silly little sectarians, their
noses had been quite put out of joint by the splendors
of the day's events) . . . all agreed, a *most* satisfactory Day of Sacrifice, Ceremony, and Festival. Piety
(represented by Paganism) and Patriotism (represented by the newly appointed Sub-Imperial-sub-
Legate of HIMSELF THE AUGUST CAESAR,
Princeps, Dux Imperatorque etc. etc., a.k.a. Lucian
the Liberator—very soon to be deified) was, locally,
at least, safe.

For the time being.

However long that might be.

And, seated in his chair of office, all sorts of official tunics and togas and straps and swords and
bundles of rods and axes and shields and eagles and
the gods knew what-all-else piled up round about
him, including (as a gentle, perhaps, hint) a neat
heap of receipt forms for sundry sorts of taxes, sat
Peregrine. He was still either in a state of shock, or at
least one of confusion, or else in one so like either
other one as to make no difference. One thing alone
was certain. He was perplexed. And so he now asked,
aloud but really intended not for the citizens who
filed past to bow before him—for him*self*—and
without at all realizing that he was asking the same
question so very often asked throughout the long,

long day by Sir Zosimus Sulla:

"What comes next?"

Perhaps no one heard him . . . that is, far off in his cavern of dreams perhaps *Gaspar* heard him . . . right then and there, though, perhaps no one but the Quæstor heard him; but hear him the Quæstor did. And the Quæstor, if he did not precisely bow, the Quæstor leaned . . . and he leaned close, very close to Peregrine's ear. And the Quæstor said, "Why, that is, must, and will be as Your Honored Excellency pleases . . ."

Late that night, after a nice hot dip in The Baths and all the rest of it, and after inscribing both their own names and titles plus his own name and titles on each silver tassy and presenting one to him, Peregrine, and promising him that the other should be safely sent demned safely and demned expeditiously, by Jove! to his old father the King of Sapodilla, late that night they two old knights lay at rest in their tent. Sir Zosimus, halfway between the hour that the ox brays in his stall and the hour when the cock crows on his roost, half-awoke, and, in a hoarse and croaking voice, half-cried aloud, "*Slagim, pusme, snata!*" Sir Rufus, with a crisp oath ("Pismo Krapuvius!" perhaps), threw a sandal at him; and, with a single smothered snortle of "Arsma*hamo*!," he returned to full sleep.

But in his own and new abode—new in the matter of his occupancy of it—where the mice ran in and out between the mouldering old chests, the mosaics clattered loosely underfoot on the humpy floor, and the stars shone with immense and immemorial indifference through the rents in the roof where old tiles had fallen off, Peregrine, before finally falling off to sleep, had remained for long and long awake.

And still perplexed.

Had he given thought (which he had never yet, this whole short journey since leaving Alftown) to King Bert's privy pouch, which the kindly King of Bertland had lent him for purposes of comparing its contents with the contents of any dragon's nest he might encounter—so as not to confuse same with the nest of, say, a crocodile or a bustard—given thought enough, even, to have checked what it contained (instead of merely taking the pouch for granted, so far had his thoughts been from it) wrapped in a wad of scarlet-dyed tow: to wit the very same dragon's egg (minus the mimworms) which the King of the Berts had won from the King of the Alves at game and yet had kindly lent to Peregrine, and which had for the most part of this recent journey lain snuggly settled in the pouch, under Peregrine's left (or shield) arm . . . and, hence, snuggled warmly . . . Had Peregrine done any of this, at least very, very recently, he could not have but observed and noticed that the aforesaid egg (provenance before Alftown to him unknown) no longer lay as inert as any egg-shaped stone, but now had begun a gentle rocking back and forth, and to emit very soft but very definite little sounds.

As though something small, inside, was tapping, to get outside.

And, had Peregrine done so, would he have been not even more perplexed?

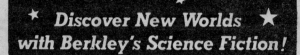